CHASING VERMEER

BY
BLUE
BALLIETT

ILLUSTRATED BY
BRETT
HELQUIST

SCHOLASTIC INC.

New York   Toronto   London   Auckland   Sydney
Mexico City   New Delhi   Hong Kong   Buenos Aires

ISBN 0-439-37297-6

We gratefully acknowledge the following institutions for permission to reproduce the work of Johannes Vermeer van Delft (1632-1675) in this book: *The Lady Writing*, The National Gallery, Washington, D.C., and *The Geographer*, Städelsches Kunstinstitut, Frankfurt, both images courtesy of Arothek in Weilheim, Germany.

Chasing Vermeer is a work of fiction. While some of the settings in Hyde Park are actual, others have been altered or invented.

12 11 10 9 8 7 6   6 7 8 9/0

Printed in the U.S.A.   40

First paperback edition, May 2005

The display type was set in Fink.
The text type was set in 12-point Hoefler text.
Title hand-lettering by David Coulson.
Original hardcover design by Marijka Kostiw

Acknowledgments:

✘✘✘Many thanks to the hundreds of kids at the University of Chicago Laboratory Schools with whom I was lucky enough to work, and who taught me so much about thinking and seeing. I am indebted to Lucinda Lee Katz, Beverly Biggs, and my colleagues at Lab for making it possible for me to teach and write. The Mary Williams Award was a great surprise and a big help. Special thanks go to my mentor and friend Bob Strang, who introduced me to the world of pentominoes and the marvels of constructivist teaching.

✘✘✘There are various opinions on Vermeer, his work, and the actual number of paintings he created. I based the facts in this book on the research of Arthur K. Wheelock, Jr., Curator of Northern Baroque Paintings at the National Gallery of Art in Washington, D.C., and author of several fascinating books on Vermeer. I am extremely grateful to Dr. Wheelock for answering my many questions. I want to thank him, also, for his advice on the muscle power of eleven-year-olds.

✘✘✘Will Balliett, Betsy Platt, Lucy Bixby, Anne Troutman, and Barbara Engel all took the time to look at early drafts and talk about ideas, and Nancy and Whitney Balliett have been helpful throughout — thank you all so much. My agent, Amanda Lewis, steered me with the greatest skill through a number of adventures. Three cheers to my editor, Tracy Mack, whose wisdom, imagination, and belief got me where I needed to go. Thanks to Leslie Budnick, associate editor, for also putting many thoughtful hours into the manuscript, and for being available and helpful at all times.

✘✘✘I want to thank my amazing husband, Bill Klein, who has helped me in a thousand ways. This book wouldn't exist without him.

For Jessie, Althea, and Dan, my three questioners ×××B. B.

For my mother, Colleen ×××B. H.

One can't learn much and

also be comfortable.

One can't learn much and

let anybody else be comfortable.

— CHARLES FORT, *WILD TALENTS*

✖ ✖ ✖ CONTENTS

✖ ✖ ✖ CHASING VERMEER MAP KEY

1 FARGO HALL   4 KING HALL
2 DELIA DELL HALL   5 HIGH SCHOOL
3 GRACIE HALL   6 MIDDLE SCHOOL

57TH STREET

HARPER AVENUE

ABOUT PENTOMINOES
AND ABOUT THIS STORY

✖ ✖ ✖ A set of pentominoes is a mathematical tool consisting of twelve pieces. Each piece is made up of five squares that share at least one side. Pentominoes are used by mathematicians around the world to explore ideas about geometry and numbers. The set looks like this:

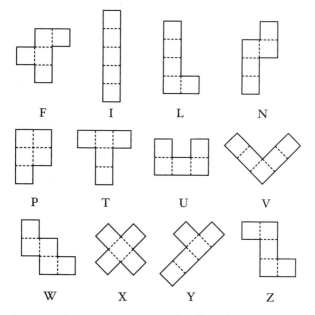

F   I   L   N

P   T   U   V

W   X   Y   Z

Pentominoes are named after letters in the

alphabet, although they don't all look exactly like their names. With a little practice, they can be used as puzzle pieces and put together into thousands of different rectangles of many sizes and shapes.

This book begins, like a set of pentominoes, with separate pieces. Eventually they will all come together. Don't be fooled by ideas that seem, at first, to fit easily. Don't be fooled by ideas that don't seem to fit at all. Pentominoes, like people, can surprise you.

ABOUT THE ARTWORK:
A CHALLENGE TO THE READER

✖ ✖ ✖ If you look carefully at Brett Helquist's chapter illustrations, you will find a hidden message. It is related to the pentomino code in the book, but not presented in exactly the same form. A certain living creature plays a part in deciphering this code, and pieces of the message appear in the artwork at regular intervals that create a pattern within the book.

Here is a hint: This pattern is even but odd. It has as many pieces as a set of pentominoes.

To check your answers go to:

www.scholastic.com/chasingvermeer

Chapter One   THREE DELIVERIES

✖ ✖ ✖ On a warm October night in Chicago, three deliveries were made in the same neighborhood. A plump tangerine moon had just risen over Lake Michigan. The doorbell had been rung at each place, and an envelope left propped outside.

Each front door was opened on to an empty street. Each of the three people who lived in those homes lived alone, and each had a hard time falling asleep that night.

The same letter went out to all three:

Dear Friend:

I would like your help in identifying a crime that is now centuries old. This crime has wronged one of the world's greatest painters. As those in positions of authority are not brave enough to correct this error, I have taken it upon myself to reveal the truth. I have chosen you because of your discriminating eye, your intelligence, and your ability to think outside of convention.

If you wish to help me, you will be amply rewarded for any risks you take.

You may not show this letter to anyone. Two

other people in the world have received this document tonight. Although you may never meet, the three of you will work together in ways none of us can predict.

If you show this to the authorities, you will most certainly be placing your life in danger.

You will know how to respond. I congratulate you on your pursuit of justice.

The letter was not signed, and it had no return address.

✖ ✖ ✖ The man had sat down to a late dinner. He liked to read when he ate, and he was on page four of a new novel. Book in hand, he answered the door.

His spaghetti and meatballs were cold by the time he remembered them. He sat at the table for a long time, looking first at the letter and then out at the moon.

Was this a joke? Who would go to the trouble of writing and sending such a letter? It was printed on expensive stationery, the kind you buy if you want to be impressive. Or pretentious.

Should he feel flattered? Suspicious? What did

this person want from him? What kind of reward were they talking about?

And who was it who knew him well enough to know he'd say yes?

✖ ✖ ✖ A woman tossed and turned in bed, her long hair trapping moonlight against the pillow. She was going over lists of names in her mind.

The more she thought, the more agitated she became. She was not amused. Could this be a coincidence, or was it a clever warning? What exactly did this person know about her past?

She finally got up. A cup of hot milk would calm her nerves. She moved carefully in the dark, using the watery rectangles of light that fell across the floor. She wasn't about to turn on the kitchen light.

The names scrolled in tidy columns through her mind, each group belonging to a different chapter in her life. There was Milan, there was New York, there was Istanbul. . . .

But this was an invitation, not a threat. If things got strange or frightening, she could always change her mind.

Or could she?

✖ ✖ ✖ Another woman lay awake under the moon, listening to the wind and the occasional whine of a police siren.

This was one of the weirdest coincidences ever.

Was this letter insane, or inspired? And was she just being gullible, thinking this person was really writing to *her*? Maybe hundreds of these letters had gone out. Had her name been picked out of a phone book?

Fake or not, the letter was intriguing. . . . A centuries-old crime. What could this person be planning?

And what about the spooky part? *If you show this to the authorities, you will most certainly be placing your life in danger.*

Maybe this was a maniac, one of those serial killers. She pictured the police going through her apartment and finding the letter, standing over her body and saying, "Jeesh, she shoulda called us first thing. She coulda been alive today. . . ."

A lone cat yowled in the alley below her bedroom, and she jumped, her heart pounding. Sitting up in bed, she shut the window and locked it.

How could she not say yes? This was a letter that could alter history.

Chapter Two <small>THE LETTER IS DEAD</small>

✖ ✖ ✖ *The letter is dead.*

It was a strange thing for a teacher to say.

By the sixth week of sixth grade, Ms. Hussey still wasn't a disappointment. She had announced on the first day of school that she had no idea what they were going to work on that year, or how. "It all depends on what we get interested in — or what gets interested in us," she had added, as if this was obvious. Calder Pillay was all ears. He had never heard a teacher admit that she didn't know what she was doing. Even better, she was excited about it.

Ms. Hussey's classroom was in the middle school building at the University School, in the neighborhood known as Hyde Park. The school sat on the edge of the University of Chicago campus. John Dewey, an unusual professor, had started it a century earlier as an experiment. Dewey believed in doing, in working on relevant projects in order to learn how to think. Calder had always liked the man's appropriate name. Not all teachers at the U., as it was called, still agreed with Dewey's ideas, but Ms. Hussey obviously did.

They began the year by arguing about whether writing was the most accurate way to communicate. Petra Andalee, who loved to write, said it was. Kids like Calder, who hated it, said it wasn't. What about numbers? What about pictures? What about plain old talking?

Ms. Hussey had told them to investigate. They took piles of books out of the library. They found out about cave art in France, about papyrus scrolls in Egypt, about Mayan petroglyphs in Mexico, and about stone tablets from the Middle East. They tried things. They made stamps out of raw potatoes and covered the walls with symbols. They invented a sign language for hands and feet. They communicated for one whole day using nothing but drawings. Now it was almost mid-October. Would they ever study regular subjects, like the other classes did? Calder didn't care. What they were doing was real exploration, real thinking — not just finding out about what a bunch of dead, famous grown-ups believed. Ms. Hussey was cool.

D-E-A-D. She had written it on the board.

They were talking about letters that morning because Calder had groaned about having to write a thank-you note, and said that it was always a waste of time. No one cared what you put in a letter.

Then Ms. Hussey asked if anyone in the class had ever received a truly extraordinary letter. No one had. Ms. Hussey looked very interested. They had ended up with a strange assignment.

"Let's see what we can find," Ms. Hussey began. "Ask an adult to tell you about a letter they will never forget. I'm talking about a piece of mail that changed their *life*. How old were they when they got it? Where were they when they opened it? Do they still have it?"

Petra, like Calder, was fascinated by their new teacher. She loved Ms. Hussey's questions and her long ponytail and the three rings in each ear. One earring had a small pearl dangling from a moon, another a high-heeled shoe the size of a grain of rice, another a tiny key. Petra loved how Ms. Hussey listened carefully to the kids' ideas and didn't care about right and wrong answers. She was honest and unpredictable. She was close to perfect.

Ms. Hussey suddenly clapped her hands, making Petra jump and setting the little pearl earring into orbit. "I know! Once you find a letter that changed a life, sit down and write *me* a letter. Write me a letter *I won't be able to forget.*"

Petra's mind was already racing.

Calder pulled a pentomino piece out of his pocket. It was an L. He grinned. L for letter — *this* letter was definitely not dead. L was one of the simplest pentomino shapes to use. Most letters, the kind you mailed, were rectangles, he realized, just like an accurately put-together pentomino solution. L was also the twelfth letter in the alphabet and one of the twelve pentominoes. Today was the twelfth day of October. Calder's grandmother had once told him that he breathed patterns the way other people breathed air.

Calder sighed. If only thoughts didn't have to be broken down into words. Too much talk was hard to listen to, and writing, for him, was a brutal process. So much got left behind.

Ms. Hussey ended the class by saying, "Got it? First find, then do. Who knows where this will take us?"

✖ ✖ ✖ Calder and Petra lived on Harper Avenue, a narrow street next to the train line. Their houses were three blocks away from the

U. School, and three houses away from each other. They often passed on the street, but they had never been friends.

Families came from all over to study or teach at the University of Chicago, and many of them lived in this part of Hyde Park. Since most parents worked, young kids traveled on their own around the campus and to and from school.

On the afternoon of October 12, Petra walked home from school with Calder half a block ahead of her. She watched him fish around for his key and open his front door. She knew his pockets were full of puzzle pieces. He sometimes muttered things and always looked like he had just woken up. He was kind of weird.

Scuffing through the first fall leaves, Petra drifted into the game she often played with herself: Ask a question that doesn't have an answer. Why was yellow cheerful, she wondered, and why was it always a surprise — even when it came in an ordinary shape, like a lemon or an egg yolk? Picking up a yellow leaf, she held it in front of her face.

Maybe she would write to Ms. Hussey about this. She'd ask her if she agreed that humans needed questions more than answers.

Calder, at that moment, looked out his front window to see Petra walking by holding a leaf several inches from her nose. He knew he was kind of weird, but she was *exceptionally* weird. She was always by herself at school, and didn't seem to care. She was quiet when other kids were loud. Plus, she had a fierce triangle of hair that made her look like one of those Egyptian queens.

Calder wondered if he was becoming just as much of an oddball. No one had asked him what he was doing after class that day. No one had told him to wait. He'd taken his buddy Tommy's presence for granted. Not now.

Tommy Segovia had lived across the street from Calder until this past August. They had been great friends since second grade, when Tommy poured his chocolate milk on Calder's bare legs and asked him how it felt. A teacher rushed over, and Calder had explained that it was an experiment and that it felt just perfect. That was the first of many collaborations.

He and Tommy had decided back in July that they weren't going to be mediocre kids. They swore that they were going to do something important with their lives — solve a great mystery,

or rescue somebody, or be so smart in school that they'd skip grades. That was the same day Calder had received his first set of pentominoes. A cousin in London had sent them as a twelfth birthday present, even though Calder's birthday wasn't until the end of the year.

The pentominoes were yellow plastic and clacked against the kitchen table in a satisfying, decisive way. Determined, Calder moved the shapes into one combination after another, flipping and turning them. The biggest rectangle he had put together so far was six pieces. A breeze was coming in the back door, and some mourning doves that had nested on the back porch were cooing, making that slippery, burbling sound that Calder always associated with summer in his neighborhood. Every detail of that morning with Tommy was strangely clear.

At once Calder had known what to do — the Y had to slide into the U, which had to fit next to the P. He even remembered the sequence of letters: YUP. He had gotten his first twelve-piecer, and gotten it fast. When he looked up afterward, he saw the pentomino shapes echoed in the kitchen. The hinges on the cabinets were Ls, the water faucets were Xs, the burners on the stove stood up on neat N legs. Maybe the entire world could be communicated in some kind of pentomino code, kind of like a Morse code. He knew, at that moment, that he would be a great problem-solver. Or so he told Tommy, who punched him in the arm and told him he had a swelled head. "Yup," he'd said with a grin.

Calder's head didn't feel too swelled these days. He looked at the clock. He was already late. When Tommy moved away, Calder had taken over his job at Powell's Used Books. Calder helped out one afternoon a week now, delivering books in the neighborhood or unloading boxes. With Tommy gone, it was something to do.

Calder gulped a glass of chocolate milk, stuffed a cookie in each cheek, and set off at a run.

✘ ✘ ✘ Powell's was one of Petra's favorite places; it was peaceful, and you never knew what you might find. It looked more like a warehouse than a store — books were piled everywhere, and the rooms were jumbled together in a mismatched way. Although Petra had been inside many times, it always felt like a labyrinth: One dimly lit area led to the next, and suddenly you were back where you started without knowing how you got there. No one asked if you needed help. No one frowned if you read but didn't buy.

Petra's mom had sent her to get milk and bread at the grocery store around the corner. Powell's was on the way.

Petra had just settled herself on a footstool with a copy of *Kidnapped* when she saw a long ponytail whip by.

Ms. Hussey?

Petra stood up carefully. She peeked around the corner, ready to pretend to look surprised. There was no one in sight. Petra looked across rows of cookbooks. She tiptoed carefully through the next room, past English, History, Psychology, and Pets. She only wanted to see what Ms. Hussey was reading.

Darn — the next person she saw was Calder. He was bending over a box of books, a piece of paper in his hand. Don't turn around, don't you dare turn around, Petra thought. She didn't want anyone from the class to see her spying.

She tiptoed around the next corner. Ms. Hussey was crouched by the art books. Petra couldn't see what she was looking at, but she noticed several paperbacks next to her on the floor. Agatha Christie, Raymond Chandler — Ms. Hussey moved suddenly, and Petra jumped backward.

To her surprise, Calder was right behind her. He had obviously seen what she was doing. Petra cupped her hand quickly as if to cover his mouth, but stopped before she touched him. They looked equally shocked. Calder, recovering first, peered around the corner. He ducked back in a flash.

"She's coming!"

It felt too late to do anything but hide, so they hurried out of History and into Fiction. Ms. Hussey was at the front desk now. She plopped down her books and began talking to Mr. Watch, the man with red suspenders who was usually at the cash register. They were laughing. Did they know each other?

"Can you see what she has?" Petra whispered. Calder walked quickly behind their teacher, his eyes on the counter. Ms. Hussey never turned her head.

"Murder and a big art book — *Never* something," he muttered to Petra when he returned.

Ms. Hussey left the store with her purchases.

A moment later, Petra ducked outside empty-handed, her cheeks burning.

She was furious with herself.

Powell's had always been her private hideaway, her refuge. Now she'd spoken to Calder there. She'd practically attacked him. And he'd seen her spying on Ms. Hussey.

What had she started?

Chapter Three   LOST IN THE ART

✖ ✖ ✖ Twenty minutes later, Petra opened her notebook on the desk in her bedroom. Letters. Think about letters.

The 5:38 southbound train went by Petra's window exactly three seconds before it passed Calder's. In between, it shot by the Castiglione's and then the Bixbys' — Petra had once calculated that it passed a house per second on Harper Avenue. She liked the trains. Looking out, she saw the bright shout of a red hat, a child in a purple jacket pressed against the window, a bald head just rising over a stiff rectangle of newspaper. She'd noticed that colors sometimes left their shapes when things flashed by so fast.

She wrote:

October 12

Yellow leaf: surprise.

Loud hat, square coat, bald head like moon: red, lavender, salmon.

Question: What does Ms. Hussey really want us to see?

"Petraaaa! Can you get me some TOY-let PAY-per?"

"CAA-ming!" Petra sighed heavily and got up to help her younger sister.

Petra's household was a tornado where life swirled in noisy circles. Sneakers, books, and backpacks traveled through the rooms on unseen currents, and there was always food underfoot and an old frying pan or two on the steps outside the back door. The cats and dog drank from the toilets, having despaired of getting their water bowls filled every morning, and everyone in the family talked to one another at the top of their lungs.

Petra wished that things were different. She wished that her parents would sit quietly at dinner and ask her how her day was, and that her four younger brothers and sisters would carry tissues with them instead of wiping off rivers of goo on their shirtsleeves in public. She wished she wasn't shy, that she wasn't shaped like a lima bean, and that her left ear didn't stick out farther than her right. She wished she was a famous writer already, and didn't have to go through the unfamous stage. She wished her mother wouldn't ever put baba ghanoush in her lunch box. When Denise Dodge had towered over her at lunchtime, saying, "*Eeeeeuuuw*! What's *that*?" Petra had wanted to murder her on the spot, but only came out with a pathetic "Don't you wish you knew!" As Denise moved away, Petra heard her saying loudly to her friend, "Blech! Aren't you glad *you* don't have to eat baby gush for lunch?"

The family socks basket was another thing Petra didn't like — she always ended up with one sock either too big or too small. Since no one wanted to sort all the clean socks that went on to fourteen feet every morning, the socks went straight from the dryer into a gigantic, handwoven basket, and it was every person for themselves. Each fall Petra's mom bought the same color socks for all seven of them so that, in theory, there was always a size that fit. But reality in the Andalee family was never that tidy.

Like many kids in Hyde Park, Petra was a club sandwich of cultures. Her father, Frank Andalee, had relatives from North Africa and northern Europe, and her mother, Norma Andalee, was from the Middle East. Petra didn't think much about what racial category she belonged to — her family had let go of that way of looking at things a long time ago.

She did know that for many generations on her mother's side, every first child who was a girl had been named Petra. She also knew that Petra was the name of an ancient stone city in Jordan, a sophisticated and graceful city that had risen out of the desert more than two thousand years ago. Three-quarters of its ruins were still covered with shifting sand; she liked the thought that she was named after a mysterious place of buried secrets.

The last "first daughter" had been her grandmother, who lived in Istanbul now. When she had visited Chicago a couple of years ago, she had told Petra that all of her namesakes had grown up to be very beautiful and very lucky. The younger Petra had looked doubtfully at her grandmother, who just looked whiskery and wispy, and who seemed to spend all day losing everything she needed, like her slippers or her black eyeliner or even the bathroom.

Glamour might have been easier in the past. Petra was sure that every Petra before her hadn't had to put up with thick glasses with blue-and-purple-speckled frames. And every Petra before her probably hadn't had to worry about what she was going to step on first thing in the morning — dried cranberry juice or a plastic dragon or something coughed up by the dog.

On her way to get toilet paper, Petra stepped heavily on a headless soldier. Served her right for being so nosy about Ms. Hussey.

Then Petra heard her parents arguing downstairs.

"But everyone has something to hide!" her dad was saying angrily. He was a physicist at the university, and Petra knew he'd been worried about his job. She heard her mom say something in an impatient tone, and then the words "letter" and "forgotten" and the quick, harsh sounds of tearing paper. What could this be about? Her parents hardly ever disagreed.

A forgotten letter! She wouldn't bring a family secret to school, but she had to look. When she crept downstairs later, however, the garbage was empty.

✖ ✖ ✖ Calder was in a bad mood. The letter assignment felt too hard. How could he ever write Ms. Hussey an unforgettable letter? And where was he going to find a stupendous letter now that Grandma Ranjana was gone? Good letters were no longer written. He was sure of it.

Calder's dad, Walter Pillay, was slicing eggplant in the kitchen. As he stacked the pale slices neatly next to the frying pan, he looked over at his son. Calder was sketching a fierce column of five-piece pentomino squares down the margin of his notebook.

"Anything wrong?" asked his dad.

Calder opened his mouth when the 5:38 train went by, rattling the windows, making the floor-boards bounce, and filling the kitchen with the *whoosh-whoosh* of passing steel. As Calder mouthed, "Nope," his dad grinned at him and mouthed back, "Good."

Calder, like Petra, was a hybrid kid. His dad was from India, and he had a calm way of speaking that made everything sound important. His job had to do with planning gardens for cities. Every year he brought home a new batch of plants to try out in the yard; by August, the front walk had vanished beneath a tangle of green. This year a trumpet vine leaned eagerly against a cool lily, pointy leaves fought to see who could take over the steps, purples and blood reds argued loudly with each other. It was a good yard for hiding things.

Calder's mom, Yvette Pillay, had short hair the color of an apricot and a jingly laugh that made other people laugh even when they didn't know why. She was Canadian and taught math at the university.

Calder had never seen either one of them look amazed when they opened the mail. He was suddenly tired of the whole idea. He didn't think he wanted to hear about letters. If he asked his mom and dad, they'd probably tell him too much. That was the problem with being an only child: Your parents were always paying attention to you. He envied kids whose families forgot about them once in a while.

✖ ✖ ✖ Walking down the block the next morning, Calder stirred the pentominoes in his pocket. He pulled out the P.

Funny, Petra was walking ahead of him. He was beginning to think he had been kind of lame yesterday, following her and then ruining her adventure.

He ducked into a driveway and crept through a

number of backyards. Under a lilac bush, around an old boat, then over two fences. The only way out was a raspberry patch. He dove in, yelped with pain, and burst out on the sidewalk just ahead of Petra.

"*Sheesh,* you scared me!"

"Sorry!" he said, pretending to be surprised. "You scared me, too."

Petra did not look pleased. "What were you doing?"

"Oh, Tommy and I always used to go to school this way. . . ." Feeling a stinging on his cheek, Calder wiped off some blood. Right. This conversation wasn't going the way he'd planned. They walked in silence for several minutes.

"Heard anything from Tommy?" Petra asked finally, though she'd hardly said a word to Tommy Segovia in her life.

"Not much." Calder groped madly for something to say, but everything he thought of sounded stupid. He was going to tell Petra that all the kids in Tommy's new neighborhood had crew cuts, but that was pretty nothing. His pentominoes were making a loud clacking sound.

"Hey, what do you think about Ms. Hussey?

She's let us do cool stuff so far, don't you think? I mean — cool for school." Petra, embarrassed by her accidental rhyme, looked sideways at Calder to see if he had noticed. A raspberry twig was standing upright over one of his ears. He looked like a lopsided bee. She was saying dumb stuff, but she hoped Calder would get the message: What happened yesterday in Powell's didn't need to be mentioned.

Calder was wondering if Petra had any interest in pentominoes or puzzles. Did she know what was in his pocket? Forget it — he'd sound like he was showing off if he asked her. He noticed that she had a couple of Rice Krispies stuck in her hair but decided not to say anything about that, either.

By the time they got to school, both were worn out by trying to think of something to say, and trying *not* to say what they were really thinking.

The cold cereal and the twig were still in place as they headed in opposite directions to their lockers.

✖ ✖ ✖ Ms. Hussey had looked strangely pleased when the assignment failed.

After two days of hunting, no one in the class had come up with anything worth sharing. There were several letters about distant relatives dying, school and job acceptance letters, invitations to weddings.

Ms. Hussey suggested that they go back a few hundred years.

"Like find old books of letters and stuff?" Petra asked, thinking of Powell's.

There was a wave of grumbling.

"How about paintings? All you have to do is look." Ms. Hussey said she'd noticed that art often showed what was important to people in any given time. It revealed things. Besides, she'd said with a smile, she was tired of being in school all day. It was time for a field trip.

Everyone sat up.

"Something else," she went on. "*Getting* an unforgettable letter happens once or twice in a lifetime. *Writing* an unforgettable letter is a pretty tough thing to do unless you have something very real to say. It shouldn't be artificial. Perhaps I made a mistake."

She always said the same thing after she had an idea, and always with an undercurrent of *we're-in-this-together-and-it-might-be-dangerous*: "Do you agree? Should we bag the assignment for now?"

There were whistles and cheers. Calder caught Petra's eye, and she shrugged and almost smiled. Everyone looked relieved. This year was beginning to feel either like something was very right or very wrong — it was hard to tell which.

✖ ✖ ✖ On the following Monday they took the train to the Art Institute and walked several blocks in the October sunshine. It was difficult to keep up with Ms. Hussey's bouncy stride. Calder noticed with approval that she never even looked back to see if everyone was with her; she was one trusting teacher.

After they ate bag lunches next to the bronze lions on the steps of the museum, they fanned out in the European wing.

Petra took off on her own. She passed the Degas dancers, the big painting made completely of dots, the Monet haystacks and bridges, and headed into the older works.

When she was in third grade, she'd had a baby-sitter who took her to the Art Institute once a month. The baby-sitter would sit in front of a painting, sigh a great deal, and sometimes write

things down. She'd tell Petra to stay in one area, but not to bother her.

Petra would walk around looking. Soon she began to wonder which paintings would be fun to go into, or which ones she might like to take home to her room. She thought about which of the children in the paintings she'd like to play with. Her baby-sitter gave her a pad and pencil, and Petra made lists. She once counted all the paintings with red clothing in them. Another time she secretly counted all the bare bottoms. She also counted all the hats and found 123.

Now she walked slowly from room to room, hugging her clipboard. She was sure there was a letter somewhere near an angel . . . or was it rolled up in someone's hand? They had one hour to look, and she knew she'd find something.

When Calder saw Petra disappear, he decided to follow her.

He stayed a gallery-length behind, and was so busy trying not to be seen that he barely noticed what was on the walls. Then, quite suddenly, Petra was gone.

Calder walked slowly through the next two

galleries. It was getting late. He'd better start hunting on his own.

Turning a corner, he spotted something promising. It lay on a bedside table inside a French painting by an artist named Auguste Bernard. The date was 1780. Calder looked around — he was alone. He leaned against the wall opposite the painting and began in a businesslike way to take notes.

The letter was folded up, but had a red wax seal that had been broken. He knew this meant it had been opened. The woman next to the letter was rolling her eyes, and her dress was ridiculously small for the top part of her body. Calder concentrated on the table, which also had a necklace of beads and a book with French words on it. He was copying the words down — *L'Art D'Aime* — when the wall behind him moved.

"What the —" Calder staggered backward into a dark doorway and stumbled over someone's feet.

The person gave him a sharp push. Then the two of them shot back into the brightness of the gallery. A guard strode over and grabbed Calder by the elbow.

"*Restricted*. Can't you read?" Too stunned to answer, Calder twisted around to see who had shoved him.

"What were *you* doing in there?" Petra hissed.

"How about *you?*" he snapped back.

The guard, a pink-and-gray sausage of a man, crossed his arms. "Storage room. No public allowed. Where's your school group, anyways?"

Calder and Petra walked in silence, on either side of the sausage, to where Ms. Hussey was talking with a group of their classmates.

"Here's where she turns into a regular teacher," Calder whispered behind the guard's back.

Petra glanced his way with a twinkle and a quick flash of "We'll see, won't we?"

"You in charge? Found these two in a storage room."

Ms. Hussey looked surprised, but not shocked. The kids standing around her tittered. Petra and Calder looked grim.

"Thank you," Ms. Hussey said to the sausage, making it clear that the conversation was over.

When the guard was out of earshot, Ms. Hussey smiled warmly at Calder and Petra, looking first at one and then the other. "Good thinking. Find anything?"

✖ ✖ ✖ When Denise changed seats on the train, a scrap of paper floated into Petra's lap:

CALDER AND PETRA LOST IN THE ART. FIRST A KISS AND THEN A FART!

Petra brushed it onto the floor, hoping Calder hadn't seen it. Why did kids have to be so stupid sometimes?

By the time everyone got off at Fifty-seventh Street, it was too late to go back to school. Ms. Hussey waved good-bye, and Calder and Petra started awkwardly down Harper Avenue.

"See you," Petra muttered over her shoulder as she hurried ahead and zoomed up her porch steps.

"Petra?"

"What?" Petra turned around.

"What were you doing in there?"

"Just looking. Most museums have too much stuff to have all of it hanging. So if it's not hanging, it's got to be stuck in a closet."

"Yeah, I guess Ms. Hussey would've thought that was cool, finding a letter that was off-limits," Calder said.

"That's not very nice. You don't like her?"

Calder began stirring his pentominoes around in his pocket. "I do."

Petra looked curiously at him. "You're jealous of me."

"I am *not!*"

"Admit it." Petra grinned.

"Well, just about your storeroom idea."

Petra's face closed. "Of course." Then she was gone.

What had just happened? Calder pulled out one of his pentominoes and tossed it up in the air. "I for idea," he said aloud.

Or was it I for idiot?

Chapter Four   PICASSO'S LIE

✖ ✖ ✖ Ms. Hussey had an extra gleam the next morning.

She agreed that the trip to the museum hadn't exactly worked. They'd found three religious scrolls and the letter with the red seal, but that was it. Ms. Hussey said she'd enjoyed the search. She didn't seem upset at all.

"You know, one of my favorite painters was interested in letters and made them important in a bunch of his paintings. Maybe that's why I thought we'd see more of them. Funny how you can project things."

She changed the subject, her voice suddenly businesslike. "So, what now? Have we reached any conclusions about communication?"

Petra raised her hand. "Maybe that it's hard to study. How about we work on something else to do with art?" She liked exploring the Art Institute. She was sure they could come up with another worthwhile subject to investigate.

Denise said, "I thought some of the art was pretty gross. I mean, a lot of it was gory and violent, or fat and naked, or plain old boring —

just people dressed up. I mean, you couldn't *make* me live with some of those pictures."

There was a murmur of agreement. Denise sniffed happily.

"I doubt you'll need to, Denise," Ms. Hussey said evenly, crossing her arms. Then she stood still and looked at the ceiling. When she didn't move, the room grew quiet.

"You know," Ms. Hussey said finally, "Picasso said that art is a lie, but a lie that tells the truth." She was pacing now. "Lies and art . . . it's an ancient problem. So if we work with art," she said slowly, "we'll have to figure out something else first: What makes an object a piece of art?"

Denise rolled her eyes but stayed quiet.

"Here's what I want you to do: Start by choosing one item at home that feels like a work of art to you. It can be anything. Don't ask anyone for advice — this has to be your own thinking. Describe this object for us without saying what it is. And this time, I won't let you off the hook." She grinned. "We'll read some of your ideas aloud."

Calder wondered what Picasso had meant. Was it that art wasn't exactly the real world, but it said something real?

He began thinking up other combinations of art, a lie, and the truth that made sense. It worked almost like the logical arrangements of five squares that made up each piece of his set of pentominoes. How about: Art is the truth that tells a lie? Maybe all of life was about rearranging a few simple ideas. Calder, smiling at the chalkboard, now squirmed in his chair with excitement at the thought. If he could just get to those simple ideas, with a little practice, he'd be a cross between Einstein and the mathematician Ramanujan — or maybe Ben Franklin —

"Calder?"

He was twisted sideways in his chair, his arm resting on his head. His pentominoes had somehow gotten onto his desk. He scooped them hurriedly into his pocket, but one fell to the floor.

"Calder, did you want to say something? It looked like your hand was up," Ms. Hussey said.

"I was just thinking. You know, about what Picasso said. But I'm still thinking," he finished. There was a ripple of unfriendly laughter from the class around him, and Calder could feel the back of his neck getting hot. If only Tommy had been there, he would've elbowed Calder earlier and gotten him back on target.

The bell rang. Denise stepped on Calder's pentomino piece just as he reached down to get it. Her knee hit him on the ear.

"*Ooooops!* Sor-ree I stepped on your toy!" She laughed and gave the plastic piece under her foot an extra scuff. It shot under Ms. Hussey's desk.

"Sor-ree your feet are so big," Calder heard Petra muttering behind him. Not sure he'd heard right, he turned to look for Petra, but she was gone.

Calder groped around for his pentomino as his teacher erased the board. He wanted to tell Ms. Hussey that he'd been thinking about important stuff, but he didn't know how to say it.

Ms. Hussey turned toward him and smiled. "I know, Calder. I get caught up in my own ideas, too. Maybe one day I'll try having us all write down daydreams for a week and see what we come up with. Maybe we'll decide they're a lot more important than what I thought we were supposed to be working on."

Calder nodded gratefully. Ms. Hussey was the best.

As he wiped off his pentomino piece, he looked at the T shape. T for what? Trouble . . . but why trouble?

✖ ✖ ✖ There was nothing at home that felt like a piece of art.

Petra considered an embroidered pillow, but it had a big tear in it; she found a silk caterpillar kite, but it had lost one eye; she thought of the stick her mom used to make a bun for her hair, the one with amber on it, but it had been missing for days.

What *was* art, anyway? The more she thought about it, the stranger it seemed. What made an invented object special? Why were some manmade things pleasing and others not? Why wasn't a regular mixing bowl or a spoon or a lightbulb a piece of art? What made certain objects land in museums and others in the trash?

She guessed that most people who went to museums didn't ask that question. They just believed that they were looking at something valuable or beautiful or interesting. They didn't do any hard thinking about it.

She wasn't going to be that kind of a person — *ever*.

She thought about pictures at the Art Institute that made her feel as if she could leave everything predictable behind. She always felt that way when she stood in front of Caillebotte's *Rainy Day* painting — the wet cobblestones underfoot, the people going places in their long skirts and top hats, the inviting turn of the street. This was art that was an adventure. It let her into another world. It made familiar stuff seem mysterious. It sent her back to her life feeling a little different, at least for a few minutes.

She was still thinking about Caillebotte's Paris street on her way to the grocery store. If he had painted Harper Avenue, would it have looked just as intriguing? As she approached the corner, she noticed the man with suspenders, the one who had talked to Ms. Hussey, step out the front door of Powell's, look around, and drop a book into the giveaway box outside. She sped up.

The book had a cloth cover with several dark stains, and the paper was thick and creamy, soft at the edges. The title jumped out at her: *Lo!* The illustrations were done in black and white — distorted, rubbery figures clutched each other or screamed.

She read a few paragraphs:

TERRIFIED HORSES, UP ON THEIR HIND LEGS, HOOFING A STORM OF FROGS.

FRENZIED SPRINGBOKS, CAPERING THEIR EXASPERATIONS AGAINST FROGS THAT WERE TICKLING THEM.

STOREKEEPERS, IN LONDON, GAPING AT FROGS THAT WERE TAPPING ON THEIR WINDOW PANES.

WE SHALL PICK UP AN EXISTENCE BY ITS FROGS.

WISE MEN HAVE TRIED OTHER WAYS. THEY HAVE TRIED TO UNDERSTAND OUR STATE OF BEING, BY GRASPING AT ITS STARS, OR ITS ARTS, OR ITS ECONOMICS. BUT, IF THERE IS AN UNDERLYING ONENESS OF ALL THINGS, IT DOES NOT MATTER WHERE WE BEGIN, WHETHER WITH STARS, OR LAWS OF SUPPLY AND DEMAND, OR FROGS, OR NAPOLEON BONAPARTE. ONE MEASURES A CIRCLE, BEGINNING ANYWHERE.

I HAVE COLLECTED 294 RECORDS OF SHOWERS OF LIVING THINGS.

What? Petra flipped back to the front and saw that the book had been written in 1931 by a man named Charles Fort.

She tucked it under her arm.

Chapter Five WORMS, SNAKES, AND PERIWINKLES

✖ ✖ ✖ That night, flipping around in *Lo!*, Petra was more and more amazed. She had never seen a book like this. It was, first of all, peppered with quotes from journals and newspapers around the world — there was the *London Times,* the *Quebec Daily Mercury,* the *New Zealand Times,* the *Woodbury Daily Times,* the *New York American, The Gentleman's Magazine,* the *Ceylon Observer* . . . the list went on and on.

There were hundreds of stories of bizarre happenings, many of them similar. Venomous snakes dropped into backyards in Oxfordshire, England; red and brown worms fell with snowflakes in Sweden; bushels of periwinkles fell from the sky on Cromer Gardens Road, outside Worcester, England; luminous, floating lights traveled slowly over open land in North Carolina and in Norfolk, England. Wild animals turned up where they shouldn't have. People disappeared and then were found far away, disoriented and confused. There were crashes and explosions that no one could explain.

Fort had apparently spent twenty-seven years

going through old newspapers in libraries. He had copied out thousands of articles about unexplained goings-on.

IT IS THE PROFOUND CONVICTION OF MOST OF US THAT THERE NEVER HAS BEEN A SHOWER OF LIVING THINGS. BUT SOME OF US HAVE . . . BEEN EDUCATED BY SURPRISES OUT OF MUCH THAT WE WERE 'ABSOLUTELY SURE' OF. . . .

Petra read this twice and turned a few pages.

I HAVE NEVER HEARD OF ANY STANDARD, IN ANY RELIGION, PHILOSOPHY, SCIENCE, OR COMPLICATION OF HOUSEHOLD AFFAIRS THAT COULD NOT BE MADE TO FIT ANY REQUIREMENT. WE FIT STANDARDS TO JUDGMENTS, OR BREAK ANY LAW THAT IT PLEASES US TO BREAK. . . . WE HAVE CONCLUSIONS, WHICH ARE THE PRODUCTS OF SENILITY OR INCOMPETENCE OR CREDULITY, AND THEN ARGUE FROM THEM TO PREM-ISES. WE FORGET THIS PROCESS, AND THEN ARGUE FROM THE PREMISES, THINKING WE BEGAN THERE.

Petra struggled with this language and had to look up the words "credulity" and "premises."

Rereading each sentence in pieces, she began to get a grip on what Fort was saying: Depending on how you looked at things, your world could change completely. His thought was that most people bent over backward to fit everything that happened to them into something they could understand. In other words, people sometimes twisted what was actually in front of them to fit what they thought should be there, never even realizing they were doing it. People liked to see what they were supposed to see, and find what they were supposed to find. It was quite an idea.

And then:

SEE LONDON NEWSPAPERS, AUGUST 18TH AND 19TH, 1921 — INNUMERABLE LITTLE FROGS THAT APPEARED, DURING A THUNDERSTORM, UPON THE 17TH, IN THE STREETS OF THE NORTHERN PART OF LONDON.

Farther down:

THERE HAVE BEEN REPETITIONS OF THESE ARRIVALS. . . . THERE IS AN ACCOUNT, IN THE LONDON DAILY NEWS, SEPT. 5, 1922, OF LITTLE TOADS, WHICH FOR TWO DAYS HAD BEEN DROPPING FROM THE SKY, AT CHALONS-SUR-SAÔNE, FRANCE.

Could this be true?

Why wasn't more time in school spent studying things that were unknown or not understood instead of things that had already been discovered and explained? Ms. Hussey always asked for their ideas. Wouldn't it be great to go digging for weird facts like Charles Fort did? To try to piece together a meaning behind events that didn't seem to fit?

And why wasn't this book a piece of art? She grabbed her notebook and began to write:

> This object is hard on the outside and bendable on the inside. It is the color of an unripe raspberry, and it weighs about as much as a pair of blue jeans. It smells like a closet in an old house, and it is an ancient shape. It holds things that are hard to believe. There are living creatures falling like rain and objects that float by themselves. People vanish and reappear.
>
> It is made of substances that once grew, that once bent in the wind and felt the night air. It is older than trips to the moon or computers or stereo systems or television. Our grandparents might have seen it new when they were young.

There was a woman's name in faded brown ink inside the cover. Petra wondered who else had loved this book and why it had ended up outside Powell's. Why had it been thrown away?

She would never lose it. Not ever.

Before closing the book, she looked again for that one terrific sentence: WE SHALL PICK UP AN EXISTENCE BY ITS FROGS.

✖ ✖ ✖ Hours later, under a sliver of moon, Petra was almost asleep. As she rolled over, squashing her pillow into position on top of her arm, a strange thing happened: Although her eyes were closed, she seemed to be looking at a young woman.

This person was old-fashioned. She was dressed in a yellow jacket that had dappled fur on the edges, and her hair was pulled back tightly with shiny ribbons. Dangly earrings, perhaps pearls, caught the light. She had been sitting at a table and writing; something had interrupted her. Quill pen in hand, she had paused to look up.

The woman was gazing directly into Petra's eyes. Her expression was knowing, filled with

kindness and interest, and she had the look of someone who understood without being told.

Petra found herself soaking up every detail of the image. Although the room was dark, light touched the metal fastenings on a wooden box, a fold of blue cloth on the table, the curve of the woman's forehead, the creamy lemon of her jacket. This was a calm, deliberate world, a world where dreams were real and each syllable held the light like a pearl. It was a writer's world — and Petra was inside it.

And then, as suddenly as she had appeared, the woman began to fade from Petra's mind. As this happened, Petra felt recognized, as if this person knew who she, Petra Andalee, was. It was a shocking feeling — exhilarating, shivery, true. And somehow inevitable, as if things had always been this way.

Wide awake now, Petra thought of Charles Fort. Was he responsible for the woman's visit? Had he brought them together? *Educated by surprises* . . . Fort understood what Petra had often felt: There is much more to be uncovered about the world than most people think.

If she'd had any idea *how* much more, Petra wouldn't have slept at all that night.

Chapter Six   THE GEOGRAPHER'S BOX

✖ ✖ ✖ On the day Ms. Hussey had given the art assignment, Calder went straight up to his room after school.

He sat down at his desk and pulled out his pentominoes. The W fit with the Y and the U, and the I slid in agreeably next to the L . . . the X was difficult to work into the rectangle, but it might fit here between the P and the U. . . . Pentominoes always helped him think.

He wrote down the word ART. He followed it quickly with: RTA

RAT

ATR

TRA

It wasn't what he'd meant to put on his list, but his pencil kind of took charge. He read what he'd written aloud. It was a tongue twister, he noticed with delight, aside from being almost every combination of A, R, and T.

Calder shook himself back toward the assignment. Was his weird list a piece of art? How about the old-fashioned kind of art, the kind in museums that turned up on postcards and posters in people's kitchens, the kind that they'd been talking about in school today? Ms. Hussey was always saying, "Listen to your own thinking." Well, what if *he,* and not those museum people, was the one to decide what was wonderful to look at? What would he choose? The same stuff that was now famous? Probably not the French lady with the too-small dress.

Art, for him, was — something puzzling. Yes. Something that gave his mind a new idea to spin around. Something that gave him a fresh way of seeing things each time he looked at it. What was he remembering?

He crawled under his bed and dragged out a dusty crate filled with green army men. He dug down into the corner and pulled out a small box.

Calder held the box carefully in both hands. It was made of a dark wood, and the corners were covered with inlaid silver vines. The painting on the top showed a man with ponytail-length hair leaning over a table. He was dressed in a fancy bathrobe, and his face was turned thoughtfully toward a window. A tool that resembled a compass was held lightly in his right hand. A large roll of paper lay under his right arm. There was a wrinkled

Oriental rug bunched up on the corner of the table in front of him, and his left hand rested on what appeared to be a book. A globe sat high on the cupboard behind him. His expression looked as though he'd been thinking important thoughts, and something had, just in that moment, interrupted him. Calder felt a sense of understanding, of sympathy for this man. This was what he felt like when he suddenly had to pay attention in school.

Calder had always loved this picture. Reaching for his magnifying glass, he held it over the top of the box. He saw light sparkle from the old glass in the window, and the rug came alive with blues and warm golden tones. On the tall cupboard was written the word "Meer." Meer, Meer . . . he rolled the word around in his mind. He wished Grandma Ranjana had told him more.

He tried to remember exactly when she had given him the box. He had been small enough to sit on her lap and play with her reading glasses — he might have been four or five. He could remember her blue velvet rocker, the cracks on her knuckles, her gentle cheeks the color of dark chocolate.

Grandma Ranjana had loved puzzles and

mysteries and would have approved of Ms. Hussey. Calder grabbed the box and rushed downstairs — he would take a "rainbow bath," as Grandma Ranjana used to call it.

On late afternoons in the fall, the sun came through the leaded glass window in the Pillays' living room and threw rainbows and wavery rhombi and polygons on the floor, the walls, the backs of chairs and sofas. This parade of soft color traveled slowly up one side of the room and vanished in the corner of the ceiling. Grandma Ranjana always swore that sitting in geometry helped the brain.

Calder began to write.

The man in my hand looks toward the window, and the light lands on one arm and one cheek and the paper on his table. You know the way paper gets blinding in a bright light? Well, this paper almost makes you squint. The colors around him are blue and red and light brown. A scrunched-up rug is on the edge of the table between him and me, as if someone tossed it up there when they were cleaning the floor and forgot to put it back.

And now for weight and size. This thing is about as heavy as a bag of chocolate chip cookies, or maybe an empty spaghetti sauce jar, or a large T-shirt. It is about as thick as a dictionary, and as long as a medium tube of toothpaste.

Calder paused, the box in his right hand, and looked at the rainbows floating on the far wall. He realized with a shiver of pleasure that the afternoon light was landing on his body in a way that was similar to the fall of light in the picture, and he wondered if he also looked like he was thinking Great Thoughts. . . .

He was interrupted by loud voices outside the front window. When he peered out, he saw Ms. Hussey and Mr. Watch, his boss from Powell's. What on earth were they doing? And then Calder noticed an old lady sitting on the ground between them.

When he opened his front door, Ms. Hussey shouted, "Water! Get some water!"

By the time he was back with a glass, the old lady was standing. Calder didn't recognize her.

Ms. Hussey said, "Thanks, Calder. I didn't

know you lived right here." She explained what Mr. Watch had just told her: He usually walked Mrs. Sharpe to Powell's once a week to pick out some books. Ms. Hussey had happened to be just behind them. She'd seen Mrs. Sharpe stumble and sink to the curb.

Mr. Watch looked embarrassed. Mrs. Sharpe looked irritated. "What would I need water for?" she snapped. "Stupid! These new shoes! A grasshopper couldn't walk in them!" Was she calling Ms. Hussey stupid?

' If so, Ms. Hussey didn't seem to notice. She offered Mrs. Sharpe her arm.

Calder went back inside and watched from his front window until he couldn't see the three of them anymore.

✖ ✖ ✖ That evening, Calder got a letter. Ripping it open, he grinned. Who else?

L:1 F:1 Z:1 N:1 P:1 T:2, -

I:2 F:1 F:2 P:1 - L:2 T:1 - Y:1 W:1 N:1 -

I:2 P:1 Z:2 V:2 - N:1 L:2 L:2 T:2 - W:1 U:2 -

T:1 T:2 L:2 U:1. - X:2 F:1 I:2 W:1 U:2 V:1 P:1 N:1 -

Z:1 F:1 U:2 V:2 - Y:2 P:1 P:1 Y:1. - W:1 -

V:2 V:1 W:1 I:2 Y:1 - Y:1 W:1 N:1 I:2 F:1 N:2 N:2 P:1 N:1. -

V:1 F:1 X:2 P:1 - V:2 L:2 - U:2 V:2 F:1 F:3 -

W:1 I:2 U:2 W:1 N:1 P:1. -

F:2 L:2 F:2 - F:1 T:1 T:2 F:1 W:1 N:1. - I:2 P:1 Y:2 -

F:3 L:2 T:2 Y:1 - U:2 V:2 W:1 I:2 Y:1 U:2. -

V:2 L:2 F:2 F:2 F:3

He hurried up to his room to dig out the pentomino code that he'd made for himself and Tommy before his friend left:

	1	2	3
F	A	M	Y
I	B	N	Z
L	C	O	
N	D	P	
P	E	Q	
T	F	R	
U	G	S	
V	H	T	
W	I	U	
X	J	V	
Y	K	W	
Z	L	X	

Calder decoded the message. Worried, he went down to the kitchen to tell his parents the news. Everyone in the Pillay household felt bad. Moving to a new neighborhood was hard enough, but having the kid next door suddenly disappear seemed like a bad joke.

Tommy had never known his real father. During the past winter, his mom, Zelda, who worked in the university library, took a vacation with two other women. They went to Bermuda. She came back with a husband.

At first, Tommy was very quiet and didn't want to talk about "Old Fred," as he started calling him. Fred tried hard to be a dad. He played baseball with Tommy in the park. He came to school and met many of the teachers. He took Tommy and Calder to Fifty-third Street for hot fudge sundaes all the time, and let them get any size they wanted. After a while, it seemed like Tommy was starting to like him.

And then Old Fred announced, last July 4 — Calder remembered the date because it took the bang right out of the fireworks — that the family would need to move to New York. He had bought a house in the suburbs without even telling Tommy's mom. "And of course not the kid," Tommy had said when telling Calder.

And now this Frog business — what kind of a name was Frog, anyway?

Calder wrote Tommy right back.

V:2 L:2 F:2 F:2 F:3, -

U:2 L:2 - U:2 L:2 T:2 T:2 F:3 - F:1 I:1 L:2 W:2 V:2 -

T:1 T:2 L:2 U:1. - F:2 F:1 F:3 I:1 P:1 - F:3 L:2 W:2 -

L:1 F:1 I:2 - U:2 L:2 Z:1 X:2 P:1 -

F:2 F:3 U:2 V:2 P:1 T:2 F:3 - F:1 I:2 N:1 -

I:1 P:1 - V:1 P:1 T:2 L:2. - I:1 P:1 -

L:1 F:1 T:2 P:1 T:1 W:2 Z:1. -

L:1 F:1 Z:1 N:1 P:1 T:2

Tommy had always liked spying; maybe this was an opportunity not to be a mediocre kid. Calder smiled, remembering their conversation in the kitchen when he had first gotten his pentominoes. He hoped his message would help.

After writing the letter and sealing the envelope, it occurred to Calder that maybe this was bad advice. What if something horrible really *had* happened to the kid next door? Whoever was responsible wouldn't want another kid snooping around. Calder's parents had told him that the chances of it being a real kidnapping were small. He hoped they were right.

Chapter Seven

✖ ✖ ✖ When Ms. Hussey read the piece of writing aloud at the end of the week, there was a shuffling and a looking-around for who seemed embarrassed or who looked too pleased.

"A strange chair?"

"Modern art with things hanging from it?"

"Does the writer want to stay anonymous, or do you want to tell us what this is?" Ms. Hussey asked after several guesses had been made.

Silence.

Petra cleared her throat. "Well, it's a special book." Petra thought suddenly of the calm, intelligent woman in her dream, the woman in the yellow jacket. *She* probably never had to explain her writing. And suddenly Petra felt the woman was sort of keeping her company, whispering, *It doesn't matter what they say. I understand.*

"A book?" snorted Denise. "Berries and smelly pants?"

Petra's mouth closed in a tight line.

Ms. Hussey turned toward Denise. "Yes. Unexpected similes can carry the power of surprise. They're refreshing, aren't they?"

Denise looked as if she had smelled something bad.

Calder was impressed by Petra's writing, and wished it were his own. An hour later, in the cafeteria, he spotted Petra in a corner by herself. He decided to join her. He wanted to tell her about the threesome outside his house yesterday, and how much he liked her description. He was imagining how surprised Petra would be to have his company.

It was then that Calder's lunch box collided with the back of a chair and popped open. Petra heard the *bang* and watched his baloney sandwich, now airborne, cross the table with impressive speed.

By the time Calder retrieved his sandwich and sat down, she had begun to laugh.

"All right, all right," Calder said.

"It's just that I was reading about inexplicable loud noises and things falling from the sky, then there was this *whop!,* and then a flying —" She was gasping. "It's not you — just so perfect —"

"What're you reading?"

"The book I wrote about. I found it at Powell's yesterday."

Calder saw that it said *Lo!* on the spine. Weird title — no wonder she was trying to cover it up.

"It's by this guy Charles Fort, who spent a lot of his life looking for newspaper articles about unexplained stuff," Petra said. "You know, like weird lights in the sky, objects traveling through rooms without any visible explanation, ghosts, crazy things like that. He talks about how blind and *idiotic* he thinks a lot of our education is. And he's funny. He doesn't take anyone's thinking too seriously, including his own." She paused, surprised at herself for saying so much. "I love hearing about people who figure things out for themselves. Plus, I love to think about things that no one understands. Yet."

"Mmm." Calder's mouth was full.

"Almost anywhere you look in here, there's something amazing. Listen to this." Petra flipped to the middle of the book.

"THERE HAVE BEEN MANY MYSTERIOUS DISAPPEARANCES OF HUMAN BEINGS. . . .

CHICAGO TRIBUNE, JAN. 5, 1900 — 'SHERMAN CHURCH, A YOUNG MAN EMPLOYED IN THE AUGUSTA MILLS (BATTLE CREEK, MICH.) HAS DISAPPEARED. HE WAS

SEATED IN THE COMPANY'S OFFICE, WHEN HE AROSE AND RAN INTO THE MILL. HE HAS NOT BEEN SEEN SINCE. THE MILL HAS BEEN ALMOST TAKEN TO PIECES BY THE SEARCHERS, AND THE RIVER, WOODS, AND COUNTRY HAVE BEEN SCOURED. . . .

"And then:

'. . . RECORDS OF SIX PERSONS, WHO BETWEEN JAN. 14, 1920, AND DEC. 9, 1923, WERE FOUND WANDERING IN OR NEAR THE SMALL TOWN OF ROMFORD, ESSEX, ENGLAND, UNABLE TO TELL HOW THEY GOT THERE, OR ANYTHING ELSE ABOUT THEMSELVES. . . .' "

Calder had stopped chewing and was staring at her.

"Tommy knows a kid called Frog, a kid in New York, who just disappeared."

"Frog?" Petra started to laugh again. "A flying frog!"

Calder kind of wanted to laugh, too, but the news wasn't supposed to be funny. What was she talking about, anyway?

"Do you believe this guy Fort?" As soon as Calder said it, he wished he hadn't. It wasn't really what he meant. Petra's face closed, and she looked disappointed.

"Well, part of what is so neat is that he worked from newspapers. I know most people would think this was completely stupid." Abruptly, Petra started to gather her things, stuffing *Lo!* into her lunch bag.

This wasn't going well. Calder *did* understand Petra's excitement; it was just that he hadn't wanted to look like an idiot again. Plus, the Frog connection had been such a weird coincidence. Before Petra could get up, he blurted, "Your writing was great, and also I saw Ms. Hussey, an old lady called Mrs. Sharpe, and Mr. Watch my boss from Powell's, outside my house yesterday. They were all there together."

Petra no longer looked unfriendly. "Mrs. who?"

"Sharpe. At least that's what it sounded like."

Petra pulled out her book again. She opened to the first page and turned it toward Calder. "Strange, huh?"

"'Louise Coffin Sharpe,'" Calder read. "Do you think that's her? I could find out," he said as if there was nothing to it.

"Okay." Petra beamed at him. "Thanks. I'd love

to know — I didn't think the first owner would still be alive."

✖ ✖ ✖ The next day was Saturday, and Calder arrived at Powell's early. Mr. Watch was seated behind the front counter, frowning over what looked like a letter.

"Ah, yes, I need you to make a delivery." Mr. Watch refolded the letter. "I'm sending you down the street with some books. The name is Sharpe."

Calder grinned. Events were fitting together now with the precision of pentominoes. He ventured, "Would that be *Louise* Sharpe?"

Mr. Watch looked stern. "Yes, but not to you." He handed Calder a paper bag filled with books.

On the way over, Calder peeked into the bag. There were some novels in French and a new book about art by David Hockney. It looked like the kind of thing Ms. Hussey would read. There was also a small, beat-up book called *An Experiment in Time*. When Calder flipped to the table of contents, he saw that Chapter Two was called "The Puzzle." Mrs. Sharpe must not be all bad.

If she recognized Calder, she didn't let on. He

decided not to remind her about the glass of water. Calder noticed that she had unusually green eyes — a sea-green surrounded by lots of wrinkles and bones. She asked him to wait in the living room while she got a check.

He looked around. He was standing on a huge Oriental carpet. Velvet cushions, naked sculpture, glass cabinets: The place was a museum. And in the corner, on a neatly organized desk, sat a large, fancy computer.

Then he saw it. Calder couldn't believe his eyes. There, hanging over the sofa, was a big version of the painting on his box.

"Do you know what that is?" Her voice made him jump.

"I was going to ask you — you see, my grandma gave me a box with that guy, I mean that painting, on the cover, and I was going to try to find out who did it — and I just did some homework that describes it — that's so strange, isn't it?"

Mrs. Sharpe sniffed and handed Calder the check. "Well, not really. That's a print of a Vermeer painting called *The Geographer*. There must be thousands of them around."

"Oh! Who was Vermeer? I know I've heard his name, but — you know." Calder, still surprised, was warming up to the situation.

"He was Dutch, and painted in the seventeenth century." She paused, looking thoughtfully at Calder's enthusiastic grin. "I'm sure you could find a book in your school library that told you something about him."

"Wow — this is just so perfect." Calder, in his excitement, was already headed for the front door. Then he remembered Petra's book.

"Hey, Mrs. Sharpe — could I ask you a question? It's about *Lo!,* a book a friend of mine, Petra Andalee, found at Powell's, and — well, I think maybe it has your name in it."

Mrs. Sharpe was dreadfully silent for a moment. What was she thinking?

When she spoke, her voice was soft. "Do you understand the book?"

Calder looked up. He couldn't tell from her face whether this was a trick question. "Part of it, anyway," he lied. "I mean, we both really like the stuff about weird things happening that nobody understands — like people who disappear. And it's cool that he found all that in newspapers."

"I didn't think anybody read books like that anymore." Mrs. Sharpe looked almost human now.

Encouraged, Calder blurted, "Oh yes, all the time." Oh no — he'd gone too far.

"Come for tea one day after school. Bring your friend and we will talk about Charles Fort." Mrs. Sharpe's voice was now icy. "Four o'clock." She turned to open the door, and Calder knew he was being dismissed.

"Okay, I will. Tha —" The door shut in his face. Calder walked back toward Powell's in a daze. *My friend Petra?* He hoped she would become his friend, and fast. There was no way he'd go back to talk about that *Lo!* stuff on his own. How did he get himself into this?

✖ ✖ ✖ Monday morning was blue and white, and everything was blowing: cumulus clouds, bare branches, scraps of rubbish.

Calder stepped out his front door and saw Petra chasing a piece of paper up the block toward the Castigliones. As he watched, the paper shot skyward in a graceful loop and headed over the roof of the Castiglione's tree house and toward the train tracks.

Petra stopped. "Darn!" she said. "That letter was half-buried in your garden. I only got to read the beginning, but it said something about an old crime and art." She shrugged. "Probably just some crazy advertisement, anyway — not a real letter at all."

"I've been thinking about that Charles House book," Calder began.

"Fort." Petra tried not to smile.

"And something else." Calder took a deep breath. "Mrs. Sharpe. That *is* her book. And she's interested that we — I mean you — know about it. She wants to meet you."

Petra had stopped walking. "Seriously?"

"She wants us to have tea with her one day. She just kind of announced it." Calder looked at the tops of the trees as if they'd been invited, too. What would he do if Petra wouldn't go? Mrs. Sharpe would soon realize he'd lied about reading *Lo!*

Petra was silent for a moment. "Wait. How did you talk to her?"

Calder explained about his job at Powell's and the delivery yesterday. The rest of the walk to school they talked about coincidence, agreeing that it didn't always seem to be accidental, and

Petra shared some of Charles Fort's ideas about looking carefully at things. Calder wanted to tell her about his box, and about the coincidence of seeing the Geographer on Mrs. Sharpe's wall, but didn't — Ms. Hussey hadn't read Calder's description aloud yet, and he was hoping Petra would like it.

They agreed that there was a great deal to be figured out in the world. Petra confided that she thought Ms. Hussey might be willing to let them collect strange data the way Fort did. That is, if kids like Denise didn't wreck it for everyone.

"Maybe data about art — art and unexplained stuff!" Petra blurted.

"Petra, you're amazing." How could he ever have thought that wedge of hair was anything but brainy?

Petra's mouth twisted strangely. "You'd better read that book before you agree with me. You might not be as crazy as I am."

He laughed and stirred the pentominoes in his pocket happily. This year was getting better all the time.

✖ ✖ ✖ Calder borrowed Petra's copy of *Lo!* that afternoon. She was right: Fort was an extraordinary thinker. He looked fearlessly at occurrences that no one could explain. Even better, he looked everywhere for patterns. Calder understood the man's fascination with connecting things that didn't seem related, and he admired the way Fort challenged the experts. How could Mrs. Sharpe ever have gotten tired of such an exciting book?

Speaking of Mrs. Sharpe, he had some detective work to do.

The reproduction of *The Geographer* in his library book was clearer and brighter than the copy of the painting on his box. Behind the man was a framed map, and above that the signature **I Ver Meer**, and under that, **MDCLXVIII**. Calder counted: a thousand plus five hundred plus a hundred plus fifty plus ten plus five plus three — 1668. The artist's full name was Johannes Vermeer, also known as Jan Vermeer, and he was from the Netherlands, in northern Europe.

The book explained that no one knew for sure who the Geographer was, but that the area where Vermeer lived was a center for mapmakers. It talked about how people with money liked to hang maps on the walls of their houses to show that they were wealthy and that they thought about the world. Mapmaking was a respected profession, something between a science and an art.

Calder flipped back and forth in the book, looking at some of the other Vermeer paintings. Most of them showed people in front of a window; the Geographer's rug appeared in many of the paintings, and the same yellow jacket turned up in a number of places. The pictures made you feel as though you were peeking in at someone else's private moment. The light that came from outside made ordinary objects seem important: a quill pen, a pitcher with milk, an earring, the brass buttons that were part of a straight-backed chair. It occurred to Calder that there could be hidden information here — after all, codes involved repetition, and the same objects appeared again and again in Vermeer's work. There was the obvious geometry of windowpanes and floor tiles, and then all the pearls, baskets, pitchers, and framed maps. There was symmetry, both complete and carefully broken.

Calder read more. The book said that Vermeer died penniless when he was in his forties, and that almost nothing was known about his life. No one understood why such a fabulous painter had made only thirty-five works of art. No one knew who the people he painted were, or why he painted the things he did. No one knew how he became an artist.

Vermeer had left behind more questions than answers.

Chapter Eight A HALLOWEEN SURPRISE

✖ ✖ ✖ On the morning of Sunday, October 31, Petra overheard her dad telling her mom that he just wasn't up for Halloween.

"Frank, think of the kids." Her mom sounded tense.

Then Petra heard her dad's rumble and parts of what he said: "Sorry, honey . . . letter in the mail this week . . . you'll see . . . be over before we know it." He'd given her mom a hug.

What letter? And what had happened to the one that was torn up? *What* would be over? Did their family need money? Would they have to move? Petra suddenly longed to tell Ms. Hussey what she'd just realized: Important letters *couldn't* be talked about because they always held secrets. Ms. Hussey must never have gotten one or she'd know that.

✖ ✖ ✖ Harper Avenue was in its element on Halloween. People came from miles around to walk down the block where Petra and Calder lived, and families took pride in becoming as frightening as possible. Graves sprang up in front yards, complete with scattered bones, headstones, and shovels. Tarantulas looped from gutters, and pumpkins flashed and growled. Corpses hanging from second-story windows swung gently in the darkness. Chocolate eyeballs rolled underfoot. A mesh of webs covered bushes and porches, and crackly voices and organ music came from flower beds. For the kids who lived on the block, costumes were a big deal.

At 4:00 that afternoon, Petra was struggling to tie ribbons in her hair. Bouncy and curly, it didn't like the idea of being pulled back so tightly. Petra finally yanked out all of the ribbons and made a tight ponytail and a tidy bun. She then fastened the already-tied ribbons on with bobby pins.

Next she put on her homemade earrings. They were large white beads that hung on a hoop. She looked different, quite definitely. The train roared by outside the window, and Petra stood still, watching her earrings tremble with the vibrations.

She put on her jacket with the fake-fur collar and cuffs — she had sewn carefully trimmed pieces of an old Dalmatian costume onto a yellow sweater. She was ready. Lowering her lids a fraction of an inch and smiling a smile that was more

an idea than a movement, she looked at herself sideways in the mirror. She felt filled, at least for that moment, with the easy elegance of the writer in her dream.

✖ ✖ ✖ When Petra opened the door, there was Calder on her front porch wearing a large red letter made out of taped-together cardboard squares.

"Hi, Calder!"

"Petra —"

She suddenly wished she hadn't done all that stuff to her hair, and instinctively pulled back out of the light.

"You look like something I've seen, I mean, just like a painting —"

"I do?" Petra mumbled.

"How did you think of dressing up like her?"

"Like who?" Petra looked at Calder directly now, frowning slightly.

"The lady with the feather pen, the lady at the desk!"

Calder tried to protect his pentomino costume as Petra pulled him into her front hall. "Tell me *exactly* what you're talking about."

"Look out! Now you've bent my F," Calder said crossly. "What're you so upset about?"

"I'm sorry. It's just that you recognized my costume. You see, I dreamed about it."

"What do you mean you dreamed that painting?"

"I didn't say it was a painting. I don't know what it was."

"Weird. I have your picture at home — come over and see for yourself."

They were down Petra's steps and up Calder's in seconds.

Once inside, Calder ducked out of his F and flew up the stairs. When he reappeared, he was carrying an oversized library book. He sat on the floor and leafed quickly through the reproductions. Petra knelt beside him.

"There!"

Petra's stomach gave a sickening lurch. It was not only her costume, it was the woman in her dream. She touched the reproduction with her hand, as if to be sure it was really there. The caption next to it read: JOHANNES VERMEER, A LADY WRITING, 1665.

Chapter Nine   THE BLUE ONES

✖ ✖ ✖ Calder and Petra found three other paintings of the woman in the yellow jacket. In one, she was wearing a pearl necklace and looking into a mirror. In another, she was playing a lute. In the third, she was seated at a writing table and a maid was handing her what looked like a letter.

"You've never seen any of these before?" Calder looked worried.

"Never." Petra had taken off one of her earrings and was rolling it around on the floor.

"So how did you dream about something you didn't know existed?"

"I wonder," Petra said slowly, "if paintings that float into your mind on their own are kind of like flying frogs or disappearing people."

"Mmm . . . you mean your dream might be part of something bigger." Calder jumped up and got a piece of paper and pencil. He handed them to Petra. "Maybe we should start keeping a record of unexplained stuff."

Petra ducked her head happily over the paper. "Fine."

She began with:

Charles Fort: chief questioner, philosopher, guide

"Hey, here's something else. Did you know I made that F costume because I was thinking 'F for Fort'?"

"We'll include that."

Calder told Petra about his box, explaining the reason he happened to be looking at the book. "I wonder what made me remember that old thing, anyway? If it hadn't popped into my mind, I wouldn't have recognized *The Geographer* at Mrs. Sharpe's, and then I would never have read about Vermeer or recognized your costume."

"It's Ms. Hussey's fault," Petra said, delighted. "It all started with her find-some-art assignment. We found it, all right."

They spent the next ten minutes trying to figure out what happened when. Petra wrote:

1. Calder writes about box with Geographer on it, same day that Petra finds *Lo!*, writes about it, then dreams about woman.

2. Calder and Petra have lunch, talk about Fort.

Calder was flipping back and forth in the book. "This doesn't tell you too much about Vermeer's life. Do you think we should do some research? I've been wondering if there's some kind of secret code that no one's ever noticed before — I mean, why so many pearls and pens and button thingies?"

"Good thinking." Petra grinned.

"And maybe there's some other crazy connection with Charles Fort," Calder went on. "Some facts we might be missing."

"We could look in the high school library tomorrow."

"Great." Calder stood up and reached into his pocket. He stirred the pentomino pieces around and pulled one out.

"V for Vermeer." He smiled in a distracted way

at Petra, who looked puzzled. "A one-in-twelve chance. Think it's coincidence?"

✖ ✖ ✖ On the way to school the next morning, Petra asked Calder about the V for Vermeer business. "I told you about the woman. Now you can tell me about these pentominoes. And don't say they're just for making rectangles."

"They help me figure things out," began Calder. He looked sideways at Petra. "Promise you won't laugh."

"Why should I? What could be weirder than my dream?"

"Well, it seems like the pentominoes kind of talk to me. I'll get the feeling that they want to tell me something, and so I'll grab one, and a word will just pop into my head."

Petra was looking at Calder with interest.

"I know. It sounds like a superstitious game. And it probably is. But you're right about Charles Fort. He makes you look carefully at stuff you might have ignored before."

"I think it's cool."

Calder smiled gratefully at Petra. He should have known she'd understand.

✖ ✖ ✖ At 3:30 that afternoon, they were sitting behind a stack of books in the library.

"Let's begin with dates, okay?" Petra, writing in neat purple ink, started a new page with the heading "Facts about Vermeer."

Calder looked at the book in front of him. "Whoa! Petra! Get this: Vermeer was baptized on Halloween in 1632. That's the first fact about his life."

"Kind of spooky, don't you think? We started writing about him on the same day that his name was first recorded. There are more than three and a half centuries in between. . . ."

"Here it is," Calder went on. "Johannes, son of Reynier Jansz and Digna Baltens —"

"Wait. Spellings."

Calder paused for a moment while Petra copied the names. He went on: "His father was an innkeeper in Delft, but was also a weaver who manufactured a fine satin cloth called 'caffa.' Vermeer was an innkeeper, too, and then an art dealer. Let's see. . . . When he was twenty-one he married Catharina Bolnes. Later that year he was registered as a 'Master Painter' in the Guild of Saint Luke . . . became a director of the same guild several times . . . had eleven children. He died in 1675, at age forty-three."

Petra was writing madly.

Calder turned the page. "It looks like he died owing money, and that he wasn't really famous until about a hundred years ago. Huh. He's mysterious, I mean everything about his life is. There aren't any records of how he got started, or of what money his family lived on. Historians don't know where he worked, or who the women and men in his paintings were, whether they were friends or family or what. I read that before — almost nothing at all is known about him as a person." Calder looked up. "That's so strange, don't you think? I wonder if someone destroyed his notebooks or letters?"

Petra glanced at Calder. "It does seem suspicious. And sad, don't you think? These magical scenes that no one will ever know more about."

Calder was reading again. "You know what else? He only signed some of his paintings. I wonder why?" Calder turned the page. "I'd never have done that," he muttered under his breath.

"Let's find out more about the painting in your dream," he went on. "Here it is: *A Lady*

Writing, and it's in the National Gallery of Art, in Washington, D.C. The thing she's wearing is a morning jacket, and it has white fur around the collar and sleeves. Those big earrings are either some kind of fancy glass or pearls, can you believe it? The oyster that made those would have to have been the size of a football. That's a quill pen, of course. The same chair with the lion's-head knobs turns up in other images . . . and the same jewelry, furniture, even maps and paintings on the walls. I wonder if this is Vermeer's home."

"Must've been hard to work with so many kids." Petra was thinking about how noisy just five could be.

"Is anything making sense here?" Calder asked.

"Well, there's the Halloween thing. That's a pretty weird coincidence."

"But is there anything else we're missing? A pattern? Numbers?"

"It seems like there's too much connection here," Petra said slowly. "Like Mrs. Sharpe knowing about both Vermeer and Charles Fort, you knowing Mrs. Sharpe, me reading Mrs. Sharpe's book and having that dream right when you were reading about Vermeer, and then the costumes we both made. . . . Do you suppose that ideas overlap like this all the time, and people just don't realize it?"

"Maybe."

Outside the library, they walked several yards in silence. Calder pulled two packages of peanut M&M's out of his coat and passed one to Petra.

"Thanks," she said, surprised.

"What's your favorite?" he asked.

"The blue ones."

"Hey, how about the blue M&M symbolizes secrecy? We can start a collection and each eat one at special times as a sign of our determination to figure this out. It'll be kind of our own private thing —" Hearing himself, Calder stopped.

Petra added quickly, "It'll represent us, Charles Fort, and Vermeer. Perfect."

They decided to save the blue M&M's in Calder's box and keep it under his bed. Petra would hold on to the notebook.

At the end of Harper Avenue they stopped and both ate an M&M, agreeing that the color blue had a rare and mysterious taste.

Chapter Ten   INSIDE THE PUZZLE

✖ ✖ ✖ Calder felt restless as he stood in front of the living room window on Wednesday afternoon. It had been two days since their trip to the library. Not knowing what to investigate, neither Calder nor Petra had done any further research.

Outside, it was pouring rain. The water was running and puddling. As Calder absentmindedly watched the droplets forming and re-forming in shape after shape, an idea came to mind. Of course! It was the obvious next step. He bounded up the stairs, away from his parents talking in the kitchen, and picked up the phone.

When Petra answered, he said, "Listen, I think we should call the National Gallery and ask if *A Lady Writing* is there. You know, to find out if the painting is safe and all that."

"Why wouldn't it be there?"

"Well, I just want to be sure. Maybe Charles Fort's warping my brain, but stories about teleportation and people vanishing into thin air . . . we should check."

"I'll be right over."

✖ ✖ ✖ Neither Petra nor Calder had ever called a museum before. They flipped a penny about who was going to speak, and Petra dialed. There was a recording, with museum hours and information about shows and tours, and then finally a chance to talk to an operator. Petra held the phone at an angle so that Calder could hear, too.

"National Gallery of Art." The voice was silky, not young, and very official.

"Umm, we're calling to find out if a certain Vermeer painting is on the wall right now."

"Oh? What picture are you looking for?" Petra made a face at Calder; the voice now had that half-fake cheeriness that some adults get when talking to kids.

Petra continued, trying to sound as businesslike as possible, *A Lady Writing.*"

"Let me check my computer. If the painting is on loan, I can tell you."

Petra and Calder waited, silent, for her to come on again.

"Well, yes, the painting is traveling just now. It's in Chicago. There's going to be a show called 'Writers in Art' at the Art Institute."

Petra's and Calder's eyes widened. Calder

grabbed the phone, pulling Petra's hair in the process. There was a fierce, whispered "Ow!" followed by a muffled "Sorry!"

"Excuse me?" The woman's voice came on again.

"Do you know whether the painting is in Chicago now?" Calder was squeezing the phone receiver so hard that his knuckles stood out.

The woman on the other end hesitated. "Well, that's what the computer said. I assume so. It left Washington several days ago, and the show opens next week."

Sensing that the woman was going to ask them what they were doing, or whom she was speaking with, Calder said a quick "thank-you-good-bye" and hung up.

"Holy smokes, Petra!"

Petra nodded, silent.

"Are you thinking the same thing I am?"

She nodded again. "I'm calling the Art Institute. And this time, Calder Pillay, you're not grabbing the phone and ripping out my hair."

After a great deal of waiting and transferring to other lines, the second call told them only that a new show was going up the following week.

"Well, it could just be that we're thinking about this stuff because the painting is part of a show here, and . . . and we're just picking it up, that's all. . . ." Petra's voice trailed off.

"Yeah, but I still feel funny knowing she's traveling, don't you?" Calder said.

"Paintings travel all the time. And now we'll actually be able to see her."

"Time for a blue one."

They sat cross-legged on the floor with the Geographer between them, arguing about whether the M&M's they'd picked were the same size. They played a halfhearted game of Monopoly. Calder's mom brought them cookies on dark blue napkins covered with green frogs.

"Hey, where did these napkins come from, Mom?"

"I don't remember, but they're fun, aren't they?"

After she left the room, Calder and Petra looked at each other.

"Maybe the rain gave the frogs an excuse to drop in," Calder grinned.

"Right. Speaking of frogs, any news from New York?"

Calder had called Tommy the night before. He'd told Calder he was beginning to wonder if there was a *reason* that everyone in his neighborhood was so unfriendly — like there was some huge secret he hadn't figured out. Frog was definitely not around, and no one wanted to tell Tommy why. He admitted to Calder that he might have been a bit dramatic with the kidnapping stuff, but facts were facts: Frog was there one day and gone the next. And no one was talking.

"I feel bad not being able to help," Calder said to Petra. "Must be creepy, wondering if you'll be the next kid to go."

"Maybe your pentominoes will say something," she suggested.

Calder stirred them around. He pulled out an N. He frowned. "N for what?" Calder thought aloud. "New York? No. National Gallery? Forget it — a serious case of Vermeer on the brain."

"Yeah, it's hard to think about anything else."

✖ ✖ ✖ After school the next day, Petra raked leaves with her dad, who seemed to be in his own world lately. He never passed the food at meals.

He had forgotten to turn off the bathtub a couple of days ago. He tried to put on tiny socks from the socks basket and just looked puzzled when they didn't fit.

Now he raked over and over the same spot on the lawn. The grass was pulling up, leaving patches of bare dirt.

"Dad?" Petra had stopped working.

"Yes?"

"You okay?"

Petra's dad looked at her as if she were on the other side of a closed window. He lifted his hand in a stiff wave. "Fine!"

But Petra didn't believe him. What had happened to him? He still went off to work, but he was always distracted. She wished with all her heart she had found the letter that had started this, the one her parents had been arguing about weeks ago. There might have been something she could have done.

As her dad headed inside, she heard him mutter, "A loan. Insane."

Petra's eyes opened wide. A loan . . . The first thing she thought of was *A Lady Writing*. What was her dad talking about? Had he meant money?

Or had she heard wrong? Maybe he'd said "alone." Either way, it sounded bad.

✖ ✖ ✖ Calder made two pumpkin pies that afternoon with his mom, and played three games of solitaire. He helped his dad fold the laundry.

"Calder, I need you for something else. Come outside." Calder's dad was already in his jacket.

Calder followed him onto the front walk, noticing with interest all the papers that had collected under the dead plants in their yard. He was remembering the letter about crime and art that Petra had found there and then lost.

His dad was squinting up at the outside of the house. "It's time we repainted. Think we should keep the same color?"

"Yup," Calder said. "That's Grandma Ranjana's color, isn't it? Too bad she can't know we're keeping her choice. Why did she like red so much, anyway?"

Calder's dad laughed. "It's a long story. Something about the artist Vermeer . . . she wished he'd used more red, because she thought he was the best, but red would have made him perfect."

"Weird," Calder said quietly.

He glanced down the block and saw Petra in her yard. She had on a red hat, a smudge of bright color against the November gray.

Sometimes he wished he'd never heard of Fort or Vermeer. Events that were purely accidental were beginning to feel like they fit together, but not in a way he understood or even knew how to think about. It was one thing if you were using a handful of plastic pieces to find solutions to a puzzle; it was another if you felt like you'd fallen inside a puzzle and couldn't get out.

Chapter Eleven   NIGHTMARE

✖ ✖ ✖ At 7:30 on the morning of November 5, Calder was hunting for his sneakers. Petra was looking under the living room sofa for the hairbrush. Both reached their kitchens at the same moment.

In the Pillay household, Calder's parents were pouring juice, pulling out cold cereal boxes, and talking. Calder caught the words "tragic" and "shocking."

"What's the matter?" he asked.

In Petra's kitchen, her mom was making cheese sandwiches and talking to her dad. Petra heard her mother say, "How could a thing like this happen? I mean, whose fault is this?"

Petra read the headlines. On the front of the *Chicago Tribune,* in giant letters, were the words *"VERMEER VANISHES: IRREPLACEABLE TREASURE DISAPPEARS BETWEEN WASHINGTON AND CHICAGO."* Petra sat heavily on a kitchen chair and began to read:

A 1665 VERMEER PAINTING ENTITLED A LADY WRITING *WAS STOLEN THIS PAST*

WEEKEND WHEN IN TRANSIT BETWEEN THE NATIONAL GALLERY OF ART IN WASHINGTON, D.C., AND THE ART INSTITUTE OF CHICAGO.

THE PAINTING WAS TO BE THE CENTERPIECE OF AN EXHIBIT TO OPEN NEXT WEEK AT THE ART INSTITUTE. A LADY WRITING *IS*, ACCORDING TO CURATORS AT THE NATIONAL GALLERY, OF "ABSOLUTELY INCALCULABLE WORTH." ONE OF THIRTY-FIVE KNOWN WORKS BY DUTCH ARTIST JOHANNES VERMEER, IT IS WITHOUT DOUBT ONE OF THE MOST VALUABLE PAINTINGS TO HAVE BEEN STOLEN IN THE TWENTIETH CENTURY.

IN AN EMOTIONAL TELEPHONE INTERVIEW, N. B. JONES, THE CURATOR IN CHARGE OF ARRANGING THE LOAN, SAID, "THIS IS EVERY MUSEUM'S NIGHTMARE. THIS IS AN EXQUISITE AND FRAGILE PAINTING THAT NEEDS TO BE KEPT IN CERTAIN ATMOSPHERIC CONDITIONS. IT IS EASILY WORTH MILLIONS OF DOLLARS, BUT COULD NEVER BE SOLD ON THE BLACK MARKET. IT MUST HAVE BEEN TARGETED FOR THEFT BY AN INDIVIDUAL COLLECTOR. THIS IS A TRAGEDY OF INDESCRIBABLE PROPORTIONS."

ACCORDING TO SOURCES AT THE ART INSTITUTE, THE PAINTING ARRIVED WITH ARMED GUARDS LATE YESTERDAY AFTERNOON. WHEN IT WAS UNPACKED WITH GREAT EXCITEMENT BY A GROUP OF CONSERVATORS AND CURATORS, THE CASE WAS FOUND TO BE EMPTY. A PRINTED NOTE WAS TAPED TO THE PACKING MATERIALS. IT READ: YOU WILL COME TO AGREE WITH ME.

EVERY ATTENDANT AND ARMED GUARD WHO WAS NEAR THE PAINTING FROM THE TIME IT LEFT WASHINGTON HAS BEEN IDENTIFIED AND IS BEING HELD FOR QUESTIONING.

Petra could hardly breathe. She had to find Calder.

Calder listened to his parents read parts of the article aloud. "I knew it, I knew it," he muttered to himself.

"What's that, Calder? It's upsetting, isn't it?" Calder's dad peered at him over the paper. As Calder ran down the hall, he heard his father remarking to his mother, "Must have Spelling today."

Calder was down the steps in one leap and

running toward Petra's house. He arrived just as she stepped out. One look at each other and both knew it wasn't necessary to break the news.

They sat down on the curb at the end of Petra's walk.

"We knew it, right? We knew ahead of time!" Calder began fiercely tearing up fallen leaves.

"Yeah, but we didn't *really* know." Petra's voice was strangled-sounding. "Besides, who would've paid any attention to two kids talking about what sounds like a few coincidences?"

"There's no question now that there's something really creepy going on here, and that we're somehow mixed up in it." Calder looked at Petra directly for the first time. "I mean, how could we have just stumbled on all this stuff?"

Petra didn't disagree. "It sounds nutty to say, but I think the Vermeer woman is depending on us — kind of like she's been waiting for us to catch up."

They were both silent for a moment.

Calder stood up. "So what do we do now?"

"What Charles Fort would do. Pay attention and keep our heads."

✖ ✖ ✖ Ms. Hussey turned up at school that morning with her arm in a sling. She explained that the lights had gone out in her house the night before, and that she'd fallen. What had seemed intriguing just a couple of days ago suddenly felt sinister to both Calder and Petra: Petra's dream painting had been stolen, Petra's dad was acting weird, Calder was worried about Tommy, and now Ms. Hussey was hurt. Petra and Calder looked at each other, silently running through all the things that were going wrong. Who or what would be next?

Ms. Hussey had the newspaper under her arm, and the first thing she did was read aloud the article about the Vermeer painting. This started a discussion about art theft, and about how thieves sometimes cut canvases out of frames. Ms. Hussey told them about a theft in 1990 at the Isabella Stewart Gardner Museum in Boston. Thieves had dressed as police and had gotten the night security guards to let them in. Then they tied up the guards, turned off the alarms, and stole at least ten paintings, including a Vermeer and a Rembrandt. Those paintings were still missing. She told them a number of other stories about art thefts, some of the plottings ingenious and some a mess.

"We just have to hope," Ms. Hussey said, "that this thief is not a professional."

"You mean that he'll do something stupid?" Calder asked. "Something that will give him away?"

"Or that he or she will crack under the strain of it all," she said, her voice sounding tired. "I'm giving you free work time this morning — I don't feel very well."

Most of the class whispered happily or read, seeming to forget about the Vermeer. All day, a book with a full-page reproduction of the Lady was propped open against the blackboard. Calder walked by it and was surprised to realize that it was the same book they'd seen Ms. Hussey pay for at Powell's a couple of weeks earlier. The word Calder had seen on the cover hadn't been "Never" — it was part of "Netherland." Netherlandish Painting.

When he told Petra, she got very quiet. "Another coincidence," she said, her voice barely audible. "I didn't like the way Ms. Hussey said that thing about cracking under the strain — she looks like *she's* cracking."

"Think we should tell her we've been studying Vermeer, too? It might cheer her up," Calder suggested.

Petra thought for a moment. "No," she said slowly, "and I'm not sure why. I think she's in some kind of trouble, and I don't want her to think we've noticed. Otherwise, we won't be able to help." Petra looked at Calder.

"Right. She wouldn't want us to get hurt, too," Calder finished. Suddenly he remembered the pentomino Denise had kicked under Ms. Hussey's desk. It had been T — T for trouble.

✖ ✖ ✖ Walking home that day, Calder and Petra saw Ms. Hussey cross Harper Avenue and head toward Powell's. They knew exactly what to do.

Hurrying to the corner, they looked both ways. There was no one in sight; she must have gone inside.

"Maybe we can see something through the front window — Mr. Watch is usually facing the other way. If we walk in the door, she might be right there," Calder said.

Petra nodded.

They crept under the window and stood up just enough to peek over the display shelves. Ms. Hussey and Mr. Watch were talking intently, their heads close together.

It was frustrating, being so close to them and not being able to hear. Petra's and Calder's minds were racing, but in different directions. Calder was going over everything he'd seen Mr. Watch ever do that was puzzling — why did he spend so much time in the art section of the store? It seemed like he was always straightening books over there. Why had he been so friendly to Mrs. Sharpe, walking her to the store before Calder started her deliveries? And were he and Ms. Hussey friends?

Petra was wondering what had made Ms. Hussey buy that art book weeks ago, and whether it was just a coincidence. Ms. Hussey was very adventuresome. Had she gotten herself in over her head somehow? Had she really just fallen the night before? Did her injuries have anything to do with *A Lady Writing*?

Heading back down their block, Petra and Calder shared their worries. If they had turned around, they would have seen Ms. Hussey and Mr. Watch leave the store together.

Ms. Hussey was carrying a thick package under her good arm.

✖ ✖ ✖ The *Chicago Tribune* editorial board printed this unsigned letter the following morning:

Dear Concerned Art Lovers,
I am the one responsible for the temporary disappearance of A LADY WRITING. *She remains in her frame, and no harm will come to her. She will be returned when the lies that surround the lifework of Johannes Vermeer have been corrected. I have committed a crime, but in my heart I know that my theft is a gift. Sometimes bold steps must be taken to uncover the truth.*

Here lies the problem: The great master known as Johannes Vermeer painted, in truth, only twenty-six of the thirty-five paintings we now attribute to him. These "real" Vermeers were done between 1656 and 1669. How do I know this? Look for yourselves. His touch is unmistakable, his vision and originality impossible to truly reproduce.

Now tell me why we have no papers, no printed materials written by this great artist about his lifework? Why do we know so little about the man?

I believe that this is the answer: Vermeer's followers and perhaps even members of his family, those he taught and those who so greatly admired him, got hold of and destroyed his papers after his death. Then, a number of works done under his direction or influence were sold as paintings either executed by an immature Vermeer at the start of his career or by the ailing artist in his last years. Centuries went by, and Vermeer fell into obscurity.

As the master's works became more and more valuable in the twentieth century, those who owned these "earlier" and "later" paintings were, of course, uninterested in the idea that they might be in ownership of a painting done by someone else. These paintings are currently in a number of big and powerful museums, including the Metropolitan Museum of Art in New York and the National Gallery in

London. Who is now brave enough to correct these errors? Who but the public at large, those with nothing to lose?

What should you do? First you must simply go and look. Look at the reproductions in books about Vermeer if you cannot get to the museums. Ask yourself, after studying the great paintings of genius done by Vermeer during the 1660s and just before, whether these other works have the same magic, the same luminous glow, the same secretive, dreamlike power. Well, do they?

The greatest art belongs to the world. Do not be intimidated by the experts. Trust your instincts. Do not be afraid to go against what you were taught, or what you were told to see or believe. Every person, every set of eyes, has the right to the truth. These paintings will speak to you as they have to me.

When you have looked as you have never looked before, you will come to agree with me. And then the record must be set straight.

To do this, you must protest. You must be difficult and impossible to ignore. I hope you will write, by the thousands, to museum officials, to newspapers, to those in power.

When the surviving lifework of this great painter has been correctly identified, I will return A LADY WRITING.

I eagerly await your involvement. I will be setting up a Web site where you may post letters on a computerized message board. They will be kept by me, and they will be read by the world.

As for the three people who received a letter from me in October, you know who you are. I cannot thank you enough. The part you have played has been invaluable.

I congratulate you all on your pursuit of the truth.

The uproar was instantaneous and dramatic.

Chapter Twelve TEA AT FOUR

✖ ✖ ✖ The unsigned letter was reprinted in a number of major newspapers around the world. This was a first: An art scholar had become a thief and was asking the public for help.

Overnight, Ms. Hussey's classroom became a combination of museum and laboratory. The walls were soon plastered with reproductions of Vermeer paintings, and library books were piled on every surface. The kids borrowed powerful magnifying glasses from the science department, trying to see how the floor tiles Vermeer painted in the 1660s compared with those in the 1670s, or whether a hand in one painting was similar to a hand in another. They studied wrinkles, reflections, shadows, wood, glass, and fabric. In the process, they discovered how blurry most reproductions can become when examined through a magnifying glass. Ms. Hussey seemed happy with the noise and argument and made everyone defend their opinions. Calder's job was to organize the data the class collected into a giant chart. Petra's was to record some of the conclusions about which paintings were "real" and which were not. Other kids set up a voting system and tallied the results, or worked on letters that they would post on the Internet.

Talk that felt exhilarating in Ms. Hussey's classroom was nerve-racking elsewhere. Behind closed doors, those in museums or in positions of authority in the art world were deep in complicated, sometimes angry discussions. Everyone agreed that the most important issue was how to get back *A Lady Writing*. Her safety came first. They also agreed that a scholarly terrorist should not be allowed to blackmail the art establishment and endanger one of the world's greatest treasures simply to have his or her way. How could museums consider the thief's demands?

Another problem was that the letter had fired the public's curiosity and imagination. The press had, of course, fed the flames. Suddenly everyone from sports stars to taxi drivers felt entitled to share their thoughts on which work was a "real" Vermeer painting and which wasn't. There were interviews every day on the news. People talked confidently about Vermeer — in fancy restaurants, in subways, in doughnut shops, in elevators. There was a wave of rebellious feeling against those who were experts in the field. After all, if art wasn't for the people of the world, who was it for? And, as the thief had pointed out, wasn't one set of eyes as good as any other? What did an education and a fancy degree have to do with seeing? The letters that swept over the Internet were adding up in the thousands.

Many were siding with the opinions of the thief. Some even forgave him or her in the interest of truth, feeling that the thief had a very important mission that would have pleased Vermeer himself.

On the day her class voted on the attribution of each of the thirty-five paintings, Ms. Hussey was oddly quiet. The majority of sixth graders sided with the thief, concluding that Vermeer's early and late works were indeed suspicious.

Impatient to know what Ms. Hussey thought, Calder asked his teacher the question she usually asked them: "Well, do you agree?" He thought she'd be pleased.

"We'll see," Ms. Hussey said in a flat, grown-up tone. It wasn't like her at all.

As she turned away, Calder thought she looked frightened.

✖ ✖ ✖ Several long weeks had gone by since Mrs. Sharpe had invited Calder and Petra to tea. In that time, *A Lady Writing* had vanished. She was gone, but she was everywhere — she was still Petra and Calder's secret, but she was now a familiar face to many thousands of others.

Mrs. Sharpe had left a message for Calder at Powell's. He and "his friend" were expected for tea on Monday, November 22.

As they walked slowly toward the house, the kids agreed that Mrs. Sharpe was a good person to be seeing. If she liked both Fort and Vermeer, she might have some insights on the theft.

Calder noticed the top of Mrs. Sharpe's head, just the crescent of a tidy white bun, in one window. It was getting dark outside, and the lighted interior looked like a painting. Through the wobble of old glass they could see the edge of *The Geographer* over the sofa, a fan of rosy light on the ceiling, a lace curtain — and then abruptly, as if in response to their curiosity, a hand reached up and released the blinds.

"Calder? Something's funny here."

"What do you mean?"

Before Petra could answer, Mrs. Sharpe opened the door. "So you're the young woman who has my book. Hurry up, you're letting in the cold air. We're having tea in the kitchen. I hate any kind of mess, so that is where we will eat."

Mrs. Sharpe ignored Petra's murmured comments about how nice the house was, saying only, "Watch your step, and don't touch anything."

Calder was thinking to himself that Mrs. Sharpe was rude. For someone who was so proper, it seemed odd. She had barely said hello.

The kitchen walls were decorated with Delft tile, and the plates in the glass cabinets were also blue and white. An old wooden table filled the middle of the room. Its surface, worn with age, glowed a buttery yellow. The chairs were large and heavy and had lions' heads carved on the tops of the backs. On the table sat a tray with a teapot, cups and saucers, and a plate with tiny chocolate cakes. There were embroidered napkins. In the

center of the table, in an earthenware jug, was a bunch of red tulips.

"Why, it's Vermeer's world!" Petra was touching the tile on the counter, running her fingers over the cobalt glaze with obvious delight.

"Sit down, both of you. You're not here to admire things." Mrs. Sharpe's voice was true to her name. Perhaps realizing how harsh she sounded, she went on in a softer tone, "We're here to talk about Charles Fort. This young man tells me you picked up my copy of *Lo!* at Powell's. But don't say anything until you've finished eating."

Calder and Petra sat down and sipped obediently on tea served in cups so thin that you could see the shadow of your finger on the other side of the china. Calder's swallowing made a loud noise in the silence. Petra wanted to giggle, but instead choked on her cake and had to wash it down with a scalding gulp of Earl Grey.

"So. Charles Fort. What do you two make of him?"

Petra cleared her throat. "He believes in figuring out the truth, no matter what anyone else says. Calder and I like that. I mean, he's such a fearless thinker."

"Yes . . ." Mrs. Sharpe was looking at Petra with an intensity that wasn't at all comfortable.

Petra looked over at Calder for help. "Calder and I have been pretty inspired by — well, by his way of seeing. It seems like most people aren't brave enough to question things the way Fort did."

"Yes. His ideas have meant a great deal to me." Mrs. Sharpe looked coldly at her teacup as if it had spoken instead of her. It occurred to Petra that maybe the old woman had said more than she'd meant to. But before Petra could think up an appropriate response, Calder blurted, "Then why did you get rid of your book?"

As soon as he'd spoken, he knew he'd made a mistake. Trying to chat with Mrs. Sharpe was not easy. It was kind of like playing with a dangerous animal.

"I was finished with it." Mrs. Sharpe's tone made it clear that she could soon be finished with Calder, too. There was another silence. "It has a dreadful stain on it, if you haven't noticed. All of Fort's books have just been beautifully reprinted in one volume, so I now have that."

Calder remained judiciously silent.

Petra stirred more sugar into her tea. "You

must like Vermeer. Horrible news about the theft, isn't it?"

Mrs. Sharpe's face was masklike. "Charles Fort would have been pleased."

Petra looked shocked. "Why?"

Calder thought he understood. "You mean pleased about all the *questions,* right?"

Mrs. Sharpe made a noise kind of like a snarl. Calder, aware that he had trespassed again, looked down at the table. He was moving too fast — what was wrong with him?

Petra tried to make things better. "Pleased about how people are thinking for themselves?"

Calder pulled a pentomino out of his pocket and began tapping it nervously against his knee. For a long minute, everything was silent.

"I think the thief is very intelligent," Mrs. Sharpe said.

Both Calder and Petra looked at her.

Calder couldn't restrain himself. "Sure he's smart, but so what? Does that make the theft okay?" There was a long silence, and Calder could feel Mrs. Sharpe's eyes drilling into his head.

"I think, as Charles Fort does, that people don't look carefully enough at what is around them." Mrs. Sharpe stood up, signaling that tea was over.

As they followed the old woman silently through the house, Petra and Calder absorbed as much of what was around them as they could. A pewter pitcher . . . several tapestries . . . goblets made of green-and-bubbly glass.

"We must talk soon. I'll leave word with Mr. Watch." The door was shut before Calder and Petra could reply.

They stood outside in the twilight looking at each other. Calder was still holding what he now realized was the F pentomino.

"For someone who obviously loves Vermeer, she didn't seem too upset," Petra said.

Calder frowned. "You know what my pentomino just said? *Fooled.* If she wasn't so old, I'd wonder if *she* had something to do with the painting disappearing."

"What reason would she have for stealing it?" Petra asked. "Plus, can you imagine her hiring a bunch of criminals to do the dirty work? But what she said about people not seeing what was right in front of them — that did feel almost like a hint."

They walked several steps in silence.

Calder was scratching his chin with the F pentomino. "You think that it's Mrs. Sharpe who's fooled, or us?"

✖ ✖ ✖ Calder got another letter from Tommy that evening. Something else had gone wrong, something besides Frog's disappearance:

L:1 F:1 Z:1 N:1 P:1 T:2, -
T:1 T:2 P:1 N:1 - L:1 F:1 W:2 U:1 V:1 V:2 -
F:2 P:1 - Z:1 L:2 L:2 Y:1 W:1 I:2 U:1 - T:1 L:2 T:2 -
L:1 Z:1 W:2 P:1 U:2 - L:2 I:2 - T:1 T:2 L:2 U:1. -
U:1 L:2 V:2 - F:2 P:1 F:1 I:2. - V:2 L:2 L:2 Y:1 -
F:2 F:3 - I:1 W:1 Y:1 P:1. - F:2 L:2 F:2 -
F:1 I:2 N:1 - T:1 T:2 P:1 N:1 -
T:1 W:1 U:1 V:1 V:2 W:1 I:2 U:1. -
                              V:2 L:2 F:2 F:2 F:3

Calder felt partly responsible — it had been his idea that Tommy do some detective work, and now his buddy had gotten in hot water because of it.

Suddenly Calder felt guilty that he and Petra were sharing secrets while Tommy was on his own. He'd always told Tommy everything. It wasn't that he'd meant to leave Tommy out. It was just that so much had happened without him.

He decided to call his old friend. There wasn't the same privacy on the phone as in their letters, but at least they could make a few jokes.

Calder got a recording saying that Tommy's number had been disconnected. A shiver of fear ran down his spine.

He dialed Petra's number and told her the news. "I can't help remembering Fort's stories about people who vanished into thin air, sometimes from the same area. You don't think this could be anything like *that,* do you?"

Petra's voice was subdued. "No, but guess what? My dad just left on a business trip and wouldn't tell my mom where he was going. He wasn't mad or anything, but said he couldn't tell her right away. He hasn't been acting like himself at all lately. He kind of disappeared, too."

Both were silent for a moment. Calder was the first to speak. "Got the Vermeer notebook?"

"Of course."

"Can you add something about our tea with Mrs. Sharpe? And maybe even Tommy's letter and the disconnected phone, and your dad's mysterious trip? You know the way writing things down sometimes makes stuff clearer."

"Good idea. Come over, okay?"

Before Calder got there, Petra looked at their last entry in the notebook. It said, *Unknown: Do objects and people repeat because V. painted at home?* Then she remembered. They'd been wondering if the women who kept turning up in Vermeer's paintings were his family, surrounded by the everyday stuff of their lives.

Absentmindedly, Petra underlined "objects and people repeat." People repeat. Who was the woman in *A Lady Writing*? Suddenly, it all felt so sad, not only the theft but the thought that the woman didn't have a name. Unknown. She was hidden somewhere in the dark, in danger and alone. Petra shut her eyes. As the first tear rolled down her cheek, she could suddenly picture the woman looking at her, her earrings shimmering in that clear light. *Don't worry,* she seemed to be saying. *I remember you, and I'm right here.*

Petra opened her eyes and sat up straight. She blew her nose. But where are you? she asked silently, feeling excited but kind of silly. Imagining a safe place to hide a small painting, she thought of drawers, cupboards, cabinets, closets, blanket chests. . . . Everything she pictured was wood. And then Petra felt an odd certainty: It was dark wood they were looking for.

By the time Calder turned up, she was writing madly in the notebook.

"Calder! I think we just might have a clue!"

She explained that the Lady had kind of helped her think of it. She wanted Calder to understand that.

Calder shrugged. "It's a logical idea, you know? Dark wood equals fancy places. The thief is an educated person, maybe with a lot of money — he or she could easily live in a mansion with old cabinets or something. Good thinking."

Petra wrote: *Look for wooden storage places in Chicago.*

Of course, there was Mrs. Sharpe's house, but neither remembered seeing anything that might fit that description in the living room or kitchen.

"Maybe we can get a look at more of her house when we go back. I'll make up an excuse about using the bathroom and run upstairs," Calder suggested. "Or maybe she'll want something from Powell's before then."

They laughed nervously about how furious Mrs. Sharpe would be if she caught them spying. "We'd be the next to vanish, you can count on it," Calder added.

Both felt better by the time they had a blue one and closed the notebook. There was comfort in making plans.

Chapter Thirteen X THE EXPERTS

✖ ✖ ✖ The next morning, they had another surprise. This one came from Ms. Hussey.

She asked her students to think about what they might have done if the thief had written them a personal letter before the theft took place, a letter delivered to their home.

"You mean like one of the three letters the thief talked about?" asked Calder.

"Not necessarily. We're just inventing a situation," Ms. Hussey answered, with some of her old *we're-in-this-together-and-it-might-be-dangerous* tone.

Hearing the undercurrent of excitement, her class grew quiet.

Ms. Hussey went on to explain that this letter would have asked anonymously for their help. Say the thief had offered lots of money, promised that the cause was honorable, and — last but not least — threatened their life if they showed the letter to anyone else.

Petra scribbled Calder a quick note: The letter that blew away from me that day on Harper Avenue — it sounded just like this! Except I didn't get to finish it and don't remember the threat.

As Calder read Petra's note, Ms. Hussey was saying, "This is a question of judgment. It's not clear, in your letter, if the thief is good or bad. I'm interested in what you might do. And Calder, could I keep that, please? You know I don't allow those kinds of communications during class."

Calder flashed an *uh-oh* look at Petra, who had slumped down in her seat. He stepped carefully over Denise's outstretched foot as he handed Ms. Hussey the note. She popped it in her pocket.

Although she knew Ms. Hussey wouldn't be angry, Petra had a queasy feeling. How could the letter Ms. Hussey was asking them to imagine sound so similar to that one about art and crime? But maybe this was just another coincidence, pure and simple — there had been so many lately. Or maybe Ms. Hussey had found the letter blowing around, too! Of course — the thought was a relief. Petra sat up.

Ms. Hussey wrote some of their responses on the blackboard:

— *Go directly to the police and get protection.*

— *Hide the letter and try to figure out who the writer was.*

— *Change the locks on the doors.*

— *Do what was asked, have an adventure, and hope you weren't breaking the law.*

— *Tell a friend and make them promise not to tell, and then talk about what to do.*

Ms. Hussey listened closely to what the kids were saying, as she always did. At the last suggestion, her eyes suddenly filled with tears. Then, just as quickly, they were gone, and she was muttering something about dirt in her eye.

Out in the hallway, Calder looked upset. He said to Petra, "Do you suppose Ms. Hussey got one of the three letters, and dropped it or something and you picked it up? What if she's kind of looking for help by asking us what we think?"

"But why would the thief ask *her* to help him? I mean, she's just a sixth-grade teacher." Petra's voice sounded unsure.

"Good people sometimes get caught in bad things." Calder was thinking now about Tommy, about Frog, about Petra's dad, about Vermeer himself.

Should Ms. Hussey be added to the list?

✖ ✖ ✖ As if he or she were playing on Petra and Calder's fears, the thief resurfaced the next morning. A full-page ad appeared in newspapers around the world.

After the thief's first published letter, the fuss over *A Lady Writing* had been tremendous. The catchy phrase *You will come to agree with me,* the message found inside the packing box after the painting was stolen, had been picked up everywhere. It appeared spray-painted on subway cars, on walls, and on the sides of buildings in New York City, in Chicago, in Tokyo, in Amsterdam. It turned up on cheap T-shirts in English, Dutch, French, Spanish, even Japanese. Demonstrations were organized outside several museums, and protestors were photographed marching and shouting. There was footage on the evening news of signs that said things like: TELL THE TRUTH! GET HER BACK! Or X THE EXPERTS! Or ¡VIVA VERMEER! ¡SOLAMENTE LA VERDAD! Museum officials had days when they had to scurry,

protected by police, through noisy crowds to get to work.

It was after this first wave of passion began to die down that the first full-page ad appeared.

It said simply: *You are doing the right thing.* Sure enough, the response from the public was instantaneous. There was more mail, there was more publicity.

The next time the public seemed to be losing interest another message appeared, saying: *Be patient. Do not give up.* This also was followed by a flood of letters.

The ad that Calder and Petra read before school that morning in the *Chicago Tribune* said: *You have come to agree with me. They will come to agree with you.*

In tiny print below the letter, newspaper editors, under pressure from the FBI, the police, and a committee of museum directors, explained that they would not publish any more of the mysterious advertisements. This was the last. The first advertisement was mailed from New York a week after the theft, the second from Florence a week after that, and the third from Amsterdam.

The thief almost seemed to be showing off, thumbing his nose at the authorities.

Ms. Hussey said nothing to Petra that morning about the note she had pocketed the day before. Maybe she hadn't even read it, Petra thought with relief. Class began with a discussion about the thief's latest ad.

Ms. Hussey asked, "Why do people assume the thief is just one person? I mean, couldn't this be a group?" She was absentmindedly twisting her ponytail around and around one thumb.

Calder raised his hand. "Don't the police think three other people are helping?"

"I don't know," Ms. Hussey said. "Do they? I guess it depends on what is considered helping. And whether those three letters even exist."

She looked so genuinely concerned that Petra and Calder began to wonder if they had jumped to silly conclusions the day before.

One thing was clear to the sixth graders: In spite of their discussions earlier in the year with Ms. Hussey, the letter as a form of communication was very much alive.

Chapter Fourteen FLASHING LIGHTS

✖ ✖ ✖ Calder arrived at Powell's that afternoon just as Mr. Watch was folding the top closed on a large paper bag. He nodded to Calder and began lettering **S-H-A-R** with an indelible marker on the outside.

Before Calder could say anything, Mr. Watch pointed toward a massive pile of children's picture books. "Need to be shelved." He turned back toward the bag and added **P-E**.

"But I'd like to deliver that," Calder blurted. "I mean, she's nice," he added lamely. Nice? he thought to himself. Hardly.

Mr. Watch stood up and adjusted his suspenders. "I can drop them off myself after work."

Calder looked miserably at the picture books. When Mr. Watch went to use the bathroom, Calder rushed over to the bag and peeked inside.

They didn't look like the kinds of books most people would bother with. There were several on the history of mathematics, a book called *On the Plurality of Worlds,* and another called *The Roots of Coincidence.* Calder heard the toilet flush and hurriedly closed the top of the bag. Funny that Mrs. Sharpe was also thinking about coincidences.

He worked extra quickly on shelving the picture books and returned to the front desk. Mr. Watch was surprised and gave him a smile that revealed a row of small, pointed teeth. No wonder the man usually kept his mouth closed.

"Need that delivery now?" Calder asked.

Mr. Watch shrugged. "Fine," he said, then reached into his pocket as if to find something. "Wait — no, never mind. Go ahead."

Calder hurried south on Harper Avenue. Should he stop at Petra's and let her know where he was going just in case something happened? No, that was ridiculous.

When the door opened, Calder was surprised to see Mrs. Sharpe looking almost friendly. The wrinkles in her face were arranged into something that resembled a smile.

"Come in while I get a check for you, boy."

Calder was left to look around again for several moments. This woman had money, no doubt about it. What did she do all day? Calder noticed a hefty pile of papers next to her computer. They were too big to sit on her desk and had their own

foldout table. Maybe she was a writer. A writer and a thief?

When Mrs. Sharpe returned, Calder shifted his weight from one foot to the other, hoping she'd get the hint. She paused to look at his feet, as if there were something wrong with them. Calder took the plunge. "Mrs. Sharpe, would it be possible for me to use your bathroom? I'm not feeling well."

Mrs. Sharpe waved a bony hand behind herself. "Up the stairs, turn left." Then she gave Calder a hawklike glance, as if to say, *I'm old, but not that old.*

Calder, sweating already, scurried up the stairs. They creaked horribly under his boots. Once at the top, he paused, trying to take in as much as possible. Sure enough, to his right, he saw a large standing wardrobe. A perfect storage place, it looked almost identical to the one behind the Geographer in Vermeer's painting.

Mrs. Sharpe's voice came from downstairs. "The switch is high, inside the door."

"Got it," Calder called back, fumbling on the wall inside the first room he came to. The light went on in a huge bedroom. There was another wardrobe with carved panels, this one covering most of the far wall.

"Oops," Calder called down, trying to sound lost. He was back out in the hall, the bedroom light off. Ah — the bathroom. Calder shut the door, flushed hurriedly, and took several deep breaths.

On his way down the stairs, he noticed a built-in cabinet with heavy doors beneath an old bench on the landing. The house was nothing but wooden storage places.

"Thanks, Mrs. Sharpe," Calder said, realizing he probably didn't have to overdo it on not looking well. He stuffed the check in his pocket. "See you soon."

The front door was closed almost before he was out of it. The old woman clearly wasn't big on good-byes.

Calder went directly to Petra's and invited her back to his house. It was quieter there, and they had to get his discoveries written down. Petra carried the Vermeer notebook.

On the way over, she said happily, "My dad just got home. He was doing some kind of research for his department. Strange it had to be so secret, isn't it?"

"Not so strange," Calder mumbled. "Secrets seem almost normal these days."

Together they sat on the floor in Calder's room. First, Petra wrote down the titles of the books Calder remembered from Mrs. Sharpe's bag, then Calder sketched the standing wardrobes. They each ate several blue ones before there was a knock at the door.

"Calder, a letter for you." His dad gave them a quick smile. "Looks like another one from Tommy."

Calder tore it open and began decoding as Petra watched, fascinated. "How did you learn to do that?" she asked.

"I made it up," he said, glad she'd happened to see. Then he began to understand what he was reading. It said:

```
L:1 F:1 Z:1 N:1 P:1 T:2, -
T:1 T:2 P:1 N:1 - F:2 L:2 X:2 P:1 N:1 -
L:2 W:2 V:2. - Y:2 P:1 - Y:2 F:1 I:2 V:2 - V:2 L:2 -
L:1 L:2 F:2 P:1 - V:1 L:2 F:2 P:1. - I:1 W:2 V:2 -
I:2 L:2 - F:2 L:2 I:2 P:1 F:3. -
                              V:2 L:2 F:2 F:2 F:3
```

"Whoa! Petra, there's something else we've got to do — we've got to rescue Tommy."

✖ ✖ ✖ Calder and Petra spent most of the weekend baking brownies and selling them on Harper Avenue. They explained to the neighbors that they were raising money for Tommy Segovia and his mom, Zelda, to come home because Tommy's new stepfather had deserted his family in New York. "There one day, gone the next," was Calder's way of putting it. Everyone was sympathetic, and everyone bought.

Late Sunday afternoon, as the grand total of $129 was being stuffed into several coffee cans to go to the bank, there was news about the theft.

The news was local.

According to the evening broadcast, an elderly woman in Chicago had just notified the authorities about receiving a strange delivery. That delivery was a letter that arrived back in October, and that woman was Louise Coffin Sharpe. She was asking for police protection.

"WHAT?" shouted Petra and Calder together. They dropped the jar of quarters they'd been counting and rushed around the corner to where

Calder's parents were watching TV in the next room.

The broadcaster read the letter aloud. Petra and Calder stared at each other. It sounded exactly like the letter Ms. Hussey had described to her class. The broadcaster explained that "For an older woman living on her own, it had required an act of great courage" to finally take the letter to the police. The broadcaster clearly had never met Mrs. Sharpe.

"Oh my God — the letter was delivered right down the block." Calder's mom clapped her hand to her forehead. "And Calder, you were just over there!"

"Mrs. Sharpe *is* involved," Calder said to Petra in a low voice. "Do you think she was waiting all that time for the thief to get back in touch with her?"

"Who can tell? And think of Ms. Hussey's letter — this can't be pure coincidence," Petra said. "It's too close."

"Do you remember that Louise Sharpe's husband was a Vermeer scholar?" Calder's dad said to his mom.

"*What?*" Calder and Petra asked in one voice.

Calder's dad said he remembered hearing that Mrs. Sharpe's husband had been murdered in Europe many decades ago, and that he had been doing research on Vermeer at the time of his death.

Calder and Petra stared at each other.

"Murdered how, Dad?" Calder asked.

"I don't remember, but I think it was considered a random street crime, a horrible case of being in the wrong place at the wrong time. They never arrested anyone."

"Poor Mrs. Sharpe," Petra said. "Well, that could explain some of her odd behavior."

"And maybe more," Calder added.

✖ ✖ ✖ The phones rang nonstop all over Hyde Park that night. Looking out his living room window after Petra went home, Calder could see the blue flash of police cars and knew they must be stationed outside Mrs. Sharpe's house. She'd be safe, no question about that. A nagging doubt crept into Calder's mind: Could Mrs. Sharpe be so clever that she had framed herself? He wouldn't put it past her. Even though her husband had been killed, it was hard to picture her being afraid so many years later. And Ms. Hussey . . . what was going on with her? The pieces just didn't fit.

Petra, three houses away, followed the flashing lights on her ceiling, her thoughts falling into rhythm with the pulse of blue.

What about the letter she had picked up that day on Harper Avenue — had that been one of the original three? Was Mrs. Sharpe really a victim now? Was Ms. Hussey?

Petra's thoughts swirled in circles, refusing to make sense.

Chapter Fifteen MURDER AND HOT CHOCOLATE

✖ ✖ ✖ The University School was buzzing the next day. Ms. Hussey was not there, and word had leaked to the papers that she had been arrested the night before as a suspect in the theft. Her class was out of control — it took the substitute half the morning to stop the accusations and shouting.

"A *suspect*! She'd never help a criminal!"

"How do you know? Maybe she was forced into it. Remember when her arm was hurt?"

"She would have called the police right away — I know her."

"We all know her, dummy. What we don't know is what's going on."

"Somebody in this room must have called the police last night."

"No way!"

"That rat is dead meat!"

"Yeah — a memory!"

Even when they'd finally quieted down, the sixth graders glowered at one another suspiciously.

There was clearly a traitor in their midst. The substitute handed out sheets of word problems to keep everyone busy.

At lunchtime, Petra and Calder sat next to each other as usual.

"I'm worried that the letter I picked up in your garden was Ms. Hussey's, from the thief. If it was, then she wouldn't have any proof that she'd been one of the three — and who would believe me if I said I'd found it and lost it again?" Petra was pushing her grilled cheese back and forth across her plate.

Before Calder could reply, Denise leaned over. "Something the rest of us don't know about, Petra? Something you'd like to tell the police? No more secrets, now. And hanging out in Calder's garden — *really*."

Petra moved away angrily, bumping Denise's elbow by mistake as she picked up her lunch tray. Denise lost control of her butterscotch pudding, and it slithered down her leg. Slipping on the pudding, she lost her balance and landed heavily on the substitute teacher, who was sitting nearby. Petra smiled. Other tables began to giggle, and Denise told the substitute that Petra had pushed her.

Calder and a number of kids turned on Denise, and soon they were shouting. Denise turned crimson and yelled, "I hate all of you!"

The class had to stay inside during recess as punishment for bad behavior.

It was a horrible day.

✖ ✖ ✖ Hyde Park continued to make the papers. The *Chicago Tribune* had pictures of both Mrs. Sharpe and Ms. Hussey on the front page the next day, as well as the happy news that Ms. Hussey had received the same letter as Mrs. Sharpe. Ms. Hussey was released. She made a statement about having been terrified, as was Mrs. Sharpe, to do anything about the letter. Both women were given round-the-clock police protection.

There were many questions. Why would a professional thief ask an old woman and a young schoolteacher to help him or her? Why hadn't the first letter been followed by another? And who had gotten the third?

Then a reporter added to what Petra and Calder already knew: Louise Sharpe was the widow of Leland Sharpe, a Vermeer expert who had died in Amsterdam thirty-one years ago. He had written to his wife that he had made a breakthrough discovery about Vermeer's work and was then silenced before he could share it.

The possibility of his death being connected to a discovery about Vermeer changed everything. Mrs. Sharpe *could* be genuinely afraid. Petra and Calder admitted to each other that she just might be innocent. Or at least partly innocent — things with Mrs. Sharpe were never simple.

✖ ✖ ✖ "Ms. Hussey!"

When she returned the next day, her sixth-grade class crowded around, giving her hugs and stepping on her sneakers.

"How was jail?"

"Were you really scared?"

"How come you didn't tell us that was your letter?"

"We were so worried about you!"

The questions poured out, but she wouldn't

talk about either the arrest or the letter. She looked happy to be back, but nervous. Every time someone dropped a book or bumped into a desk, she jumped. She glanced into the hallway a number of times, as if afraid that the policeman on duty might have left.

She took down all of the Vermeer posters and all of the newspaper clippings. The classroom looked bare and dismal. She asked the class what they wanted to study, but when they suggested ideas, she didn't seem to be listening. Petra thought about bringing up Charles Fort's research, but could tell it wasn't the right moment.

The day after Ms. Hussey came back, Petra left science class and went to her homeroom to get a book she'd forgotten. She found Ms. Hussey standing alone, her back to the door, talking on a cell phone.

Petra took two steps into the room and froze. She overheard "mistake . . . but why . . . it *is* here . . . but I can't do that!" And then her teacher began to weep. Not wanting her to know that she'd heard, Petra crept out.

Petra felt suddenly outraged for Ms. Hussey.

She was a wonderful person. Who or what was hurting her? And were Mrs. Sharpe and Ms. Hussey really so protected now?

Petra didn't think so. Something was very wrong with Ms. Hussey.

✖ ✖ ✖ "Come on, Calder," Petra said when school ended. "Let's go someplace we don't usually go, someplace on the campus. How about Fargo Hall? I've got money for hot chocolate."

Petra's hat was pulled down almost to her eyebrows, and her hair fanned out in a black halo around the bottom. She was walking a couple of steps ahead of Calder.

"You remember what Mrs. Sharpe said about people not looking carefully enough at what is around them?"

"Of course," Calder said.

"I think we should be careful, that's all."

"What's the matter? Something happen?" Calder was looking curiously at her.

"I'll tell you when we get there."

They plodded quietly through the dim afternoon light, heading two blocks north on

University Avenue. Fargo Hall, close to a century old, had stone gargoyles and carved human heads on every turret and ledge. A tangle of leafless ivy clutched at the limestone walls.

As they pulled open the heavy doors on Fifty-seventh Street, there was a comforting blast of heat and student messiness. Petra bought two hot chocolates with whipped cream, and they headed through French doors into what looked like a giant living room. There was a fire in the fireplace, and students were scattered around in armchairs, talking quietly or reading.

They sat down on huge leather chairs in a corner.

"Here's what I'm thinking," Petra began. "You and I know some things other people don't. There're all the coincidences that have led us along, the possible storage places in Mrs. Sharpe's house, and my feeling that the painting might be hidden behind dark wood."

"Right." Calder nodded toward the walls in the room they were sitting in. "It's everywhere."

"I think we need to go into high gear and start actively hunting." Petra told Calder about overhearing Ms. Hussey's conversation. "I have a feeling that she may be in real danger. We may not have much time."

Calder put down his cup and started running his fingers excitedly through his pentominoes.

"Shh," Petra said, aware of someone glaring at them, someone in a dark armchair across the room.

Calder pulled out one of the pieces. "It's the U. U for understand . . . no, that's not right. It's U for under. Under — maybe the painting is hidden beneath something."

"What else do we have to go on?" Petra asked.

"Well, what you heard today."

". . . it *is* here . . . " Petra repeated Ms. Hussey's words.

"Here!" said Calder. "Imagine that Ms. Hussey, being adventuresome and wanting to do the right thing for art, did help the thief. Or how about this: Imagine that she and Mrs. Sharpe are working together. They do know each other. Imagine Ms. Hussey hid the painting and Mrs. Sharpe knows where it is. Imagine they picked a spot they both knew. What would be a logical place?"

"Maybe it's also U for University School! What

a brilliant place to hide something — around hundreds of kids!"

Calder was jabbing the U pentomino into the arm of his chair for emphasis. "Great — and imagine that we *found* the painting, and no one ever had to know that Ms. Hussey was involved? Except you and me, and we'd never tell. We'd be rescuing all three of them: the Lady, Ms. Hussey, and Mrs. Sharpe."

"How about the third person? The person who got letter number three?"

Petra glanced over to see that the armchair in the corner was empty.

"The dark horse — the difficult piece in any puzzle that doesn't seem to be there at all until you need it." Calder popped the U back into his pocket.

Both tried not to get too excited. Charles Fort, as Calder reminded Petra on the way home, collected "294 showers of living things" without knowing why.

Chapter Sixteen   A Morning in the Dark

✖ ✖ ✖ The University School was built around a central courtyard. Gracie Hall, now the Lower School, had been built in 1903 as a home for John Dewey's radical new school. Forming the west side of the quadrangle, King Hall had been built almost thirty years later for the University of Chicago's education department. The idea was to be able to observe what was going on in Dewey's now-famous laboratory. A new middle-school building, built in 1990, was on the east side, and the high school, built in 1960, on the north. Poppyfield Hall, tucked behind the high school, dated back to 1904 and had music and art rooms.

The following morning, Calder and Petra sat down on a bench in the Gracie Hall lobby. They were facing a stone fireplace that had a bust of Francis Parker on the mantel. Parker, a colleague of John Dewey's, had a University High baseball cap on and a red scarf around his neck.

"The painting is small, remember? The canvas is only about a foot by a foot and a half." Calder was fiddling with his pentominoes.

"Think — hundreds of kids and grown-ups go in and out of this building all day. There are cleaning people in here at night. What's a place that no one would disturb?"

Calder pulled a pentomino out of his pocket and looked at it.

They both stared at the T in Calder's palm. "T for twelve. There aren't twelve floors . . . hmm. I don't get it." Calder shrugged.

Petra sat up straight, her knees cupped in her hands. "Let's try to think like Ms. Hussey. She'd find a place with no leaks or mice or anything."

Calder was scraping the T back and forth on the wooden bench. "Twelve . . . does Ms. Hussey have twelve of anything?"

"She wears all those earrings — there's a key, a pearl, a high-heeled shoe . . ."

Calder was muttering now. "Key-pearl-shoe . . . shoe-pearl-key . . . pearl-shoe-key . . . heel-key-pearl . . . key-pearl-heel . . ."

"Hey! That sounds like 'keep her here,' doesn't it?" Petra laughed. "Now you've got *me* thinking like a pentomino. Maybe this means she's in Gracie Hall!"

Calder, in his excitement, gave Petra a quick bear hug. "Good thinking," he said.

Straightening her glasses, she tried not to look too pleased.

He and Petra agreed that they should pretend to make a master map of the school. This would give them an excuse to poke around during lunch. None of the classes aside from their own would know that it wasn't an assignment.

At lunchtime, armed with measuring tapes, clipboards, and pencils, they'd covered the first floor, checking even unlikely places. They looked in storage closets, behind file cabinets, under the beds in the nurse's office, inside old paper towel dispensers in the bathroom, around the coatrack in the director's boardroom, and beneath hats and mittens in the Lost and Found.

On day two, they covered the second floor, although it was hard to be thorough. Most of the classrooms had hundred-year-old built-in cupboards and drawers and bookshelves, and it was awkward explaining why they had to look into those to measure the room. Petra got bitten by a hamster, and in the science room Calder accidentally allowed a box of hissing cockroaches to escape down a heating grate. Petra dropped a hunk of limestone being examined by fourth-grade geologists on her toe, and Calder got a third-grade teacher angry by trying to look behind her bulletin board and knocking off some drawings of the Great Chicago Fire.

They had worked their way through Gracie Hall except for the basement, which was locked.

They decided to talk with Mrs. Trek, the Lower School principal, about letting them in. Always enthusiastic about kids' projects, she could be counted on to help. They explained about the map, and she agreed to take them down there the next day.

"That defeats the whole purpose." Calder was digging in his locker for his math book. He didn't realize that Petra had walked ahead.

A voice behind him said, "Talking to yourself? Where's your girlfriend?" It was Denise. Calder felt his face get hot and slammed his locker door. Someone ought to hide *her* somewhere — permanently.

✖ ✖ ✖ On Monday morning they met up with Mrs. Trek, as planned. Reminiscing about the kindergarten field trip to the basement, a tradition in the Lower School, Calder and Petra watched as the principal struggled with the bolt.

They had forgotten how weird the place was. The walls were fieldstone, and the floor went uphill and down. Right angles had clearly been abandoned below ground level. They saw piles of rolled rugs, broken benches, a tangle of plumbing pipes, even a claw-foot bathtub. There were spidery shapes made out of old desks stacked top to top. Mrs. Trek had just unlocked the supply room when her cell phone began to ring. A parent needed to speak with her in the office.

"Oh dear — will you be okay down here for just a minute? I'll be right back."

As soon as she left, Calder and Petra opened the supply room door. Reaching bravely into blackness, Calder groped around for the light. It wasn't on the wall by the door. He took a couple of steps into the room, ran into a string hanging from the ceiling, and pulled it. Shelves of construction paper and boxes of pencils and rulers jumped into focus. Teachers were allowed down here for supplies. Both kids could imagine Ms. Hussey using it as a hiding place.

There was no time for talking. Quickly they ran their hands along shelves, looked behind cartons, tried to lift crates. On one side of the room were several old picture frames. Behind them, leaning against the wall, was a small package wrapped neatly in brown paper. It wasn't as dusty as the others, and was the right size, no doubt about it.

They heard steps coming down the stairs and Mrs. Trek calling their names. By the time the principal reached the supply room, Petra was alone.

✖ ✖ ✖ Petra told Mrs. Trek that Calder had needed the bathroom and had gone back up. As they walked toward the stairs, Petra asked if they could return in the middle of the morning.

"I'm afraid I won't be free again until tomorrow." The principal smiled kindly as she locked the heavy metal door. "Think you can wait?"

"Sure," Petra said, her mind racing. "No problem."

As soon as she got to the classroom, Petra told Ms. Hussey that Calder had a morning dentist appointment, and slipped into her seat. She tried, but it was just about impossible to pay attention in class. She excused herself to go to the bathroom more than once, tore down to the basement door each time, and knocked softly. There was no sound from inside.

Calder stayed crouched for what felt like hours. This was the darkest dark he had ever been in. The basement didn't seem to have any windows. At one point, he heard a scurrying sound. He knew that Gracie Hall, like most old buildings in Hyde Park, had mice. And there were also those hissing cockroaches that had disappeared down a vent. He stood up.

Holding the painting carefully, he took two steps, then two more. What if there was some monster living in this basement? Someone who had snuck in when the janitor wasn't looking?

Humming tunelessly, he felt his way up the stairs. When he got to the landing, he tried the door to the first floor. The handle turned, but the door was bolted. He crept back down, trying not to touch the walls. Better to stay out of sight. Maybe, if he was lucky, someone would come down to get pencils and leave the door open long enough for him to slip out.

He reminded himself that he was probably

holding one of the greatest treasures of the art world. What were a few hours of his life next to all the adventures the Lady must have been through in her three hundred–some years? Besides, now he and Petra would be famous. They'd be interviewed on TV. They'd be in the *Chicago Tribune*. . . .

Groping his way along, he found a chair and sat down slowly. He'd better stop daydreaming. A number of things had to happen before the painting was safe — if it *was* the painting. To occupy himself, he worked on some puzzles in his head.

First he made three different twelve-piecers. Then he tried writing to Tommy, but without the code, it was tough.

Soon Calder felt himself wanting to doze. It was so quiet, and so dark.

✖ ✖ ✖ Petra hurried down to the Lower School office at lunchtime.

"Mrs. Trek isn't here, dear. She's gone for the rest of the day." The secretary looked irritated.

Petra felt a rush of determination. "The basement — my friend Calder and I need to finish an assignment by today — is there some one who could let me in?"

"We don't allow kids down there alone, you know that."

"Mrs. Trek said it was fine for us to finish our research, though," Petra lied. "She said she'd make an exception. Please. Plus, we're sixth graders."

The secretary looked at Petra and sighed. "All right. Just let me get my lunch."

While the secretary was gone, Petra looked carefully at the top of her desk. Maybe the keys were inside the drawer. If she found them, should she race down and let Calder out? If the secretary came with her, she'd discover Calder had been there all morning. It'd be better to get blamed for taking the keys.

She stepped quickly over to the desk, jerked open the drawer, and found — sure enough — the fat ring of master keys. Stuffing them into her pants pocket, she headed toward to the basement entrance as fast as she could go without looking conspicuous.

She waited outside the basement door, pretending to use the pay phone until there was no one in either direction. Her hands were fumbly and damp. First one key . . . no. Then another . . . no. Someone was coming. Petra picked up the phone again, her heart pounding wildly. She felt sure the person walking by would hear it, but they didn't stop.

The third key turned easily. Pulling open the basement door, she clicked on the switch and slipped inside.

✖ ✖ ✖ "Calder! *Calder!*" she whispered at the foot of the stairs.

There was no answer. It was too quiet. Couldn't he hear her? As her eyes adjusted to the dark, she made out a small figure slumped in a chair. The package was still held tightly in his arms. Her first thought was that he'd died of fright.

She hurried over and gave him a prod.

He popped upright. "Jeesh, Petra! I ought to get ten pounds of blue ones for being down here all this time."

"I'm glad you're all right, but hurry up, Calder! I had to steal the keys. Hurry!"

They were up the stairs, peeking out the door, and in the front hall in seconds. They clicked the basement door shut behind them. Petra grabbed a jacket from the Lost and Found box in the lobby and covered the package with it just as the secretary came around the corner carrying her lunch.

"Well, hello, you two. I'll be right back to let you in. It won't take long, will it?"

Silent, both shook their heads.

As soon as she headed off toward the office, Petra looked at Calder in a panic. "Now what? What do we do about her keys?"

"Leave them in the door to the basement. She'll think Mrs. Trek left them there."

✖ ✖ ✖ Petra and Calder were too nervous to talk on the walk home from school. They raced up Calder's front steps and straight to his room.

Both struggled with the zipper on Calder's backpack. In the rush at school, he had pulled it closed on the fabric.

"Stupid thing!" Calder grabbed scissors from his desk and cut open the backpack.

They pulled off the tape wrapped around and around the brown paper. The edges of a dark wooden frame emerged, and then an old backing. They turned it over.

Someone with an eager, pear-shaped head and a green bun sat writing at a table. Her one visible ear was graced with what looked like a dangling Ping-Pong ball. There was an orange moon behind her, and a melting castle. The painting might have been done by a second grader, a second grader who was now a grandparent.

It was not the Lady they'd been looking for.

Chapter Seventeen what happens now?

✖ ✖ ✖ Calder was home with a cold the following day, and Petra walked home from school by herself.

It was early December, and patches of ice alternated with drifts of brown leaves. Petra scuffed along, thinking about Charles Fort. *He* wouldn't be feeling discouraged. He'd have his eyes wide open. With that in mind, she picked up a scrap of graph paper off the ground and read,

corn oil
butter
tea bags
onions
green grapes
bacon

She popped it into her pocket. Was there poetry here, in these accidental combinations of words? Would Fort have seen an interesting pattern or a secret of the universe in grocery lists?

Hey — this might be something they could

get into with Ms. Hussey one day: accidental combinations of sounds and ideas. Why did some words seem more elegant, more graceful than others? Why were some words peanut butter and jelly sounds, and others caviar? What made the words "onion" or "tea bag" so plain? Why did a word like "ice" or "exquisite" sound so lacy?

Inspired by the idea, Petra spotted another piece of paper. It was tucked into a thorny hedge near Mrs. Sharpe's house, and torn along the bottom. Folded in four, it looked worn.

She opened it carefully and began to read:

Dear Friend,
I would like your help in identifying a crime that
is now centuries old. . . .

✖ ✖ ✖ Petra ran straight over to Calder's house.

"Did anyone see you pick it up?"

"I looked around — only one person crossing the street."

Calder blew his nose vigorously. "Do you think it's the same letter you started to read, the one that blew away?"

"How could it be? Maybe there's a *fourth* letter." Petra groaned.

Calder reached for his pentominoes. "It's creepy to think of someone sticking that letter carefully in Mrs. Sharpe's bushes."

"Do we tell the police? It'll make it harder for us to keep looking."

"Good thinking. But neither one of us should walk around here on our own. We could end up like that Frog kid."

They refolded the letter, placed it neatly inside a sandwich bag, and tucked it into the Geographer's box.

They each ate a blue one. Then they each ate two more.

Calder was holding the P pentomino. "P for pray," he said, trying to grin.

Petra looked horrified. "Prey?" she said. "Us? You mean we're being hunted?"

"No, I meant *pray,* as in hoping to stay safe," Calder said.

"Maybe it's *pray* we're not *prey,*" Petra added, scaring them both.

✖ ✖ ✖ The next day, more news broke. A book

appeared in the stores that morning called *The Vermeer Dilemma: What Happens Now?* Easily a fifty-dollar art book, it was being sold for an unusually affordable $1.50. This was less than the price of a Big Mac. An anonymous gift had made it possible for "everyone with an interest in Vermeer and in this painful situation" to buy the book. Written by a respected art historian, it included an excellent color plate of every painting attributed to Vermeer.

Thousands of copies changed hands across the United States on the first day, and countries around the world reported similar sales.

The book was about all the positive things that had come out of this terrible crime. People were looking at and talking about paintings as they never had before. They were comparing furniture, tile work, the structure of a leaded glass window, the folds in a satin skirt. They were comparing details, like the way light struck a fingernail or a wrist bone, the look of a woven basket handle or a curl of hair. They were examining works of art with a toughness and intensity usually seen only in the buyers of new cars or electronics. Groups of people pointing and arguing energetically in front of a Vermeer had become a common sight. Museums were busier and livelier places.

It was the first time that many "untrained" people had felt that they could say something of value about a work of art, something that might make a difference. It was the first time that many people had realized how murky and changeable the waters of history can be. When an artist leaves behind no personal papers, when hundreds of years go by, who is to say that followers or forgers didn't use his or her name to make some money? And, of course, the idea of correcting a centuries-old mistake, of pointing out that the experts in museums and universities weren't really as expert as they'd thought they were, was irresistible.

Children were thinking about Vermeer, too. They were comparing, writing, and visiting museums with friends. Many said that they hadn't realized how cool old pictures could be. They also hadn't realized that the art in museums can be mysterious, that grown-ups don't always know what it means or where it came from.

The author talked about how this uproar was probably also good for art historians and museum curators. It was forcing them to question views that had been accepted for decades, to look carefully at what they had been taught. Was the thief right? Was the public right? Why *didn't* the so-called "early" and "late" Vermeers have that luminous, haunting touch?

The book ended by stating firmly that while what the thief had done to get the attention of the art world was wrong, the public's relationship to Vermeer and to other great masters had, as a result, changed drastically. People around the world had developed a comfort with great art that they had never had before. The theft *was* a gift.

The last page carried a message to the thief. Whether or not museums chose to change the wall labels next to some of Vermeer's paintings, the public had done an amazing job of spotlighting any possible fraud. Everyone was now looking. It was only a matter of time, the author suggested, before museums would respond to the public's thinking. In the meantime, *A Lady Writing* should be returned. The thief could consider his mission to have been successful.

Chapter Eighteen   A BAD FALL

✖ ✖ ✖ Petra and Calder talked about the book on the way to school the next morning.

"All these questions being asked by people around the world," Petra said, still excited by what she'd read. "It does make the theft seem partly good."

"Yeah, but what if the thief turns out not to be as moral as he sounds — what if he's a real sicko?"

"Someone on the radio was talking about that this morning." Petra looked sideways at Calder. "But don't you think I would sort of know if the Lady had been hurt?"

They walked several steps in silence. Calder kicked at a snowbank. "Maybe. And maybe not — I wish she'd say something else to you. Like, 'Down this street, up those steps, in this cupboard, and presto'!"

They were laughing when they turned the corner near Mrs. Sharpe's house. To their horror, they found themselves facing the flashing lights of an ambulance. The children stood, mouths open, as a stretcher appeared at Mrs. Sharpe's door. The old woman was neatly strapped in under a mound of blankets. She looked tiny and pale. Two policemen followed the emergency technicians.

"Mrs. Sharpe! Are you okay?" blurted Petra.

Calder called out, "What happened?"

At the sound of their voices, the old woman turned her head. "Oh good. It's you two. Close your mouths before your tongues freeze." Mrs. Sharpe struggled to get her hand out from under the blankets. "Stop, you carriers! I want to speak with the children. I know them." Mrs. Sharpe's imperious tone brought everyone to a standstill.

"I slipped and cracked something in one leg — very stupid of me, I must say. Never broken anything in my life. I was planning to take this letter to the post office today. I could have someone in the hospital mail it, but I would prefer giving it to the two of you."

"No problem." Calder reached for the letter in Mrs. Sharpe's hand. She watched with something of her old fierceness while Calder put away the letter.

"Now, don't forget and don't lose it, boy." Mrs. Sharpe was eyeing the duct tape on Calder's backpack. "The two of you can visit me at the hospital later if you'd like. I'm sure by then I'll be stuck in some dreadful room."

"Don't worry, Mrs. Sharpe. We'll mail your letter. Want us to bring you books or anything?" Petra asked.

"No, no . . . oh, the pain of this darn leg! Stupid, stupid!" Mrs. Sharpe collapsed back on the stretcher.

"All set, ma'am?" one of the EMTs asked her politely.

"Well, yes. Does it look like we're sunbathing on the Riviera here?" Mrs. Sharpe's voice trailed off into the freezing air as she was loaded into the ambulance.

They watched it drive away. "Poor thing. I guess we won't be having tea with her anytime soon," Petra said.

"I wonder who *this* letter is for." Calder reached into his backpack and pulled it out. It was addressed, in neat handwriting, to Ms. Isabel Hussey.

✖ ✖ ✖ They held the letter up to a bright light in school. The envelope was impossible to see through.

Giving it directly to Ms. Hussey was tempting, but they had made a promise to Mrs. Sharpe. It was hard to know who to be loyal to, or what the consequences of either decision might be.

After school, they crunched through the snow to the post office on campus.

"Maybe we could steam it open," Calder suggested.

"Maybe she's just sympathizing. Maybe we're just suspicious," Petra said.

"Hey! What if we rip open the envelope and then put the letter in a fresh one? We'll just rewrite the address!"

In their excitement, they stopped and gave each other a high five.

Petra suddenly looked unhappy. "But aren't we getting pretty two-faced here? We go there for tea, we act like nice kids, and then we betray her. How would we like it if someone we trusted read our mail? This is probably how people turn into criminals. They just do something a little bit wrong, and then something a little bit worse —"

"It's not like we won't mail it afterward. We're keeping our promise. It's an emergency situation, remember? We're on a mission to rescue Ms. Hussey,

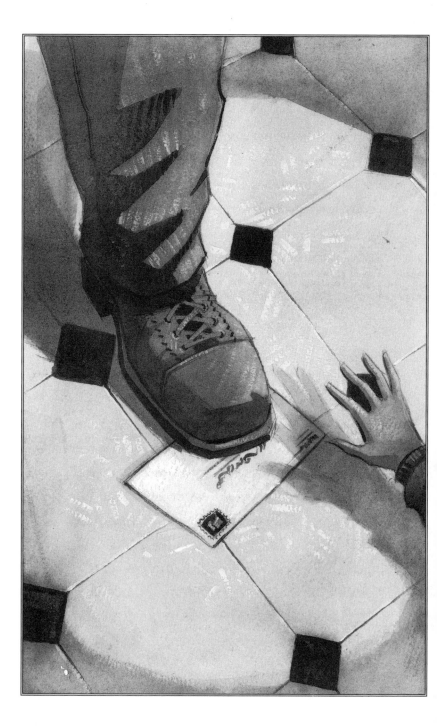

the Lady, Mrs. Sharpe, and ourselves — we may be in danger, too, now that we've got the third letter."

"So this is to protect everyone."

"Right. We're just doing a little much-needed detective work."

They were now inside, standing next to one of the slits in the wall that read: STAMPED MAIL.

"We could buy an envelope and readdress it here." Calder dug in his pockets for change.

Petra still looked worried. "What will Mrs. Sharpe do to us if she finds out? And what if Ms. Hussey recognizes our handwriting?"

"This is foolproof. We're going to put the letter in the mail the minute we've read it. Mrs. Sharpe will never know, and I'm sure Ms. Hussey will throw away the envelope."

Just then someone jostled Calder's arm, and the letter fell. Calder reached for it, and his backpack swung off his shoulder, knocking both him and Petra sideways. The letter was now under a man's leather boot.

"Ach! So sorry! Zis is going in ze mail, too?" The man then swooped the letter up in a large red paw and stuffed it into the slit along with his mail.

"I don't believe it!" hissed Calder.

Petra gave Calder a weak smile. "I guess we've been saved from a life of crime."

✖ ✖ ✖ When they arrived at the hospital, Mrs. Sharpe was lying flat in bed. One leg was heavily bandaged.

"I can't give you tea, but you can have these. They're all I could get hold of." Mrs. Sharpe handed them each a large chocolate lollipop and pushed some buttons that made the head of her bed go up. "I wanted to thank you for mailing my letter."

The three of them sat for a moment in silence.

"I suppose you're wondering what that letter was about."

Calder looked down at his lollipop. Petra swallowed loudly.

Mrs. Sharpe's eyes narrowed. "Children! *Was* that letter mailed? There is something you're not telling me."

Calder decided to come clean. "Well, you see . . . we noticed the letter was to Ms. Hussey . . . and she's our teacher, you know . . . and we've been following the thief's letters and advertisements in the *Chicago Tribune* . . . and we're working together on trying to find the Lady . . . and Petra had a dream about the Lady . . . and so we wanted to read the letter . . . we were just curious to see if you were worried about Ms. Hussey, too —"

"STOP! Did you open my letter?" Mrs. Sharpe's voice was frightening.

"No," Petra whispered. "It was my fault, too. We thought that because you're smart and you like Vermeer, you might know something about the theft, and — that you might have some good ideas. We were curious about why you wrote to Ms. Hussey. We were going to read your letter and then put it in a new envelope and mail it for you, but we didn't end up opening it. That's the truth. I'm really sorry, Mrs. Sharpe, I don't know what got into us." Petra was almost in tears.

There was a long, unbearable silence. Neither Calder nor Petra dared look up. Then a strange creaking sound came from the bed. Mrs. Sharpe was laughing. It sounded as though she was a little out of practice.

The children looked at her in amazement. "You're not angry?" Calder asked.

"Oh, not really." Mrs. Sharpe was drying her

eyes with a tissue. "I see myself in the two of you. I've done many things in my life out of curiosity, and have regretted very few of them. The important thing here is that you stopped yourselves before you did something wrong." Her face straightened. "Very wrong. The point is that you must *never* read someone else's correspondence." After allowing the children to feel uncomfortable for another few moments, she continued in a brusque tone, "My maiden name, Coffin, is from Nantucket Island, in Massachusetts, and when I read in the papers that Ms. Hussey was from there, I just thought I'd share the coincidence with her. Now. What is this about a dream?"

Grateful that Mrs. Sharpe didn't seem to be too furious about the letter, Petra started talking. She described in detail her dream about the painting, confiding that *no one* but Calder knew about it. She mentioned that Vermeer's Lady sometimes seemed to communicate with her. Mrs. Sharpe studied Petra intensely as she spoke. The old woman's eyes narrowed until they were almost slits in her face.

"Yes, she's speaking to you."

"Excuse me?" Petra's voice was almost a whisper.

"Well, there are many things about life, many experiences, that we don't have an explanation for, as Mr. Fort said. But what interests me is the idea that much of what we humans take to be a lie is true, and much of what we think is true is a lie."

Mrs. Sharpe was speaking slowly, looking at her hands. "Charles Fort would have said something to you like, 'Who's to say that art isn't alive, anyway? Who's to say what's real? If frogs can fall from the sky, why can't paintings communicate?'"

Calder had hopped up from his chair. "Petra! Remember the Picasso quote that Ms. Hussey told us about art being a lie that tells us the truth?"

"Sit down, boy. You're making my leg nervous." Mrs. Sharpe's frigid tone sent Calder back to his seat. Her face settled into an unreadable expression. "Truth . . . perhaps . . . you think you two could succeed where the FBI has failed?"

"Well, nothing happens in life unless you try. And we're pretty smart kids, you know." Calder had pulled out his pentominoes and was quietly making rectangles on the table next to Mrs. Sharpe's bed. "We haven't even told you about these."

"Smart, you think so?" Mrs. Sharpe watched Calder for a moment in silence. "What are those, boy? Some kind of new toy?"

"They're pentominoes," Calder responded with dignity. He told Mrs. Sharpe the letter name for each of the twelve pieces. Then he explained that you could make many, many rectangles out of them, but that it took practice.

"Push that table over here." Mrs. Sharpe tried putting the pieces together for a few minutes, mumbling "twelve pieces" under her breath again and again. Everyone was quiet. No rectangles appeared.

"It's hard at first. It takes time," said Calder kindly.

"Pah!" Mrs. Sharpe was looking frustrated. "I can think of something else you could do with these. How many, oh, five-letter words, say, could you make using at least three of these twelve letters in each word? Ever done that?"

"No." Both children were leaning toward the table now. Mrs. Sharpe was saying, "Let's see, the letters are F, I, L, N, P, T, U, V, W or M, X, Y, and Z. I love word challenges like these. Finds, flute, lines, filmy, tails . . ."

"Hey! That's thirteen letters. Who said the W could be an M?" asked Calder.

"I did." Mrs. Sharpe was busily pushing around the pieces.

"Wilts and tilts!" added Petra.

"Melts!" shouted Calder.

"Lower your voice, boy! We don't want one of those policemen outside the door to start bothering us. Now if you could add another letter, you could have monkey, and then there's panel . . . and vines!" Mrs. Sharpe was looking very pleased with herself, muttering, "Finds . . . fruit . . ."

At that moment, a nurse bustled into the room. "Time for your medication, Mrs. Sharpe."

"Oh, go away!" she snapped.

The nurse refused, and Calder and Petra stood up to go. As Calder picked up his pentominoes, Mrs. Sharpe nodded at them. "Wonderful tools. Could be put to many uses."

"Yes, I even like to —" began Calder eagerly.

But Petra was pulling on his arm. "We've gotta go, Calder."

Mrs. Sharpe thanked them for visiting and

waved one hand in dismissal. As they walked away, they could hear her arguing with the nurse.

✖ ✖ ✖ That night Calder got a phone call from Tommy with the terrific news that he and his mom were moving back to Hyde Park. Tommy didn't know exactly when this would happen, but he said that the Dewey Avenue Rescue Fund, the money Calder and Petra had collected by selling brownies, was a definite help. Old Fred hadn't left much behind.

Then Tommy told Calder more news: Frog had been found. His parents had gone on a long trip and left him in Washington, D.C., with a relative. No one in Tommy's New York neighborhood had been willing to tell the "new kid," in Tommy's words, what was going on — either that, or they were all so unfriendly that they didn't know or care where Frog and his family were. Tommy said he'd just gotten a postcard from the National Gallery of Art, "one of those Vermeer pictures, the stolen one," from Frog. Calder couldn't wait to tell Tommy what was going on, but knew he and Petra had to keep quiet for the moment.

He called Petra immediately. She was thrilled to hear about Tommy.

Calder went on, "Remember the N for National Gallery, that day we were trying to get the pentominoes to say something about where Frog was? That day with the frog napkins and the rain?"

"Uh-huh."

Calder filled Petra in on the rest of the story. "Makes me think of a Charles Fort thing. Frog disappears to the National Gallery, then a picture of the Lady travels back to Tommy. It's not teleportation, but some kind of strange symmetry —" Calder was quiet for a moment.

"Or some kind of weird joke," Petra finished. "Things going together that don't seem like they should."

"Things with a scary sense of humor," added Calder.

Chapter Nineteen THE SHOCK ON THE STAIRS

✖ ✖ ✖ After their visit with Mrs. Sharpe and the news about Frog, Petra and Calder couldn't wait to get back to the search.

The only remaining part of the University School compound that had paneling was King Hall. The middle school and the high school buildings were too new, and Poppyfield Hall had been carved up into studio and theater spaces.

Used only for college classes and offices, King Hall was practically empty after school. Starting on the first floor, Petra and Calder worked their way upstairs.

There seemed to be miles of dark wood. Leaving the lights out, they ran their hands along square wall panels in lecture rooms, tapping softly and looking for hidden compartments. They opened closets and cupboards, but all were empty. They leaned on grates and rattled bulletin boards. The building seemed discouragingly solid.

"This place is dead compared with Delia Dell," Calder said, looking out at the bright building across the street. Completed in 1916, Delia Dell

Hall boasted countless gargoyles and faces half-hidden in decades of ivy. There were stone turrets, an assortment of chimneys, and casement windows. In addition to the original rooms, it had a pool, a pub, and a modern movie theater. Parties and performances were held there. The building cast a warm yellow glow on the snow, a glow that sent fingers of light into the dark classrooms of King.

"So much for my U for the U. School pentomino idea," Petra said, standing next to Calder at the window. "Guess she's not here. How about a quick look in Delia Dell before we go home?"

"Sure — plus, we can get M&M's there, and I'm starving."

Their voices faded into the early darkness as they headed across the street, leaving the quiet of King Hall to resettle behind them.

✖ ✖ ✖ Calder and Petra sat on a long bench on the first floor in Delia Dell, sharing blue ones and a bag of potato chips. Snow was falling, magically softening and erasing the university world beneath it. They piled jackets and hats and gloves into a damp mound beside them.

Several college students on the other side of the room were talking about a Latin class. A man with heavy eyebrows sat reading a newspaper. A professor with a head like a pink bowling ball hurried in the direction of the pool, towel under his arm. A woman carrying a giant ring of keys passed their bench and headed up the stairs. Calder could hear the sharp *click* of a door opening, and the *thunk* of a lock sliding into place from inside.

Petra didn't seem to notice any of this. She was eating steadily, looking straight ahead of her with a sleepy expression.

Calder was feeling talkative. "Wow, this whole place is wood. Look at that staircase. I've never really noticed it before. It looks like something from an old movie — you know, like Bette Davis should be standing at the top."

"Right." Petra stood up and stretched. "Come on, it's getting late."

Away from the entrance hall, they wandered through room after empty room of paneled wood, stone fireplaces, tiled floors. They stayed in the older parts of the building.

Neither had realized how big the original part of Delia Dell Hall was. It twisted and turned gracefully, a rectangular dance with surprises in scale and mood. One moment it was grand, the next cozy. There was a huge ballroom space on the first floor, with a tai chi class going on in one corner. Across the way was a miniature reception room followed by what looked like a dining room. Plaster grapevines covered the heavy beams overhead, and the walls, paneled in rectangles of varying sizes, were interrupted here and there by almost-invisible doors. A small wooden knob and a keyhole were the only indications that something might be up. One door led to an old-fashioned kitchen, one to a back staircase, and three or four others were simply locked.

The dining area opened into a sunny library with a generous fireplace. Over the mantel, a wooden scroll read: DEDICATED TO THE LIFE OF WOMEN AT THE UNIVERSITY OF CHICAGO. Carved lions and horses flanked the dedication.

Petra stood in front of it, admiring the elaborate Gothic letters. "Cool. I wonder what that means?"

"My mom told me this was the first place at the university where women students could hang out. Anyway," Calder said, "let's keep going."

On the second floor there were some offices and three empty lecture rooms, all with rows of wooden chairs, old oil paintings on the walls, and elaborate leaded glass windows.

The third floor had a miniature theater. The walls of the room facing the theater were covered with a parade of young people in medieval costumes dancing, playing, and talking with one another in an idyllic country setting. The north wall had vaulted windows with French doors that opened onto a roof terrace. Petra and Calder stood, awed, at the entrance to the room. A red velvet curtain covered the stage, and on either side was a small wooden door.

Propelled by the same urge, they walked slowly toward the stage. There was no one in sight. Without a word, Calder tried the door on the right-hand side. It opened. Three short steps led up to a tiny backstage area.

They crept inside, stepping over frayed curtain ropes, a lute with no strings, a plastic pitcher, and an old broom.

"These look like props for a goofy Vermeer," Calder said.

He thought Petra would smile, but she didn't

seem to be listening. "Not much place to hide," was all she said.

Petra suddenly felt as though she had forgotten something important, or as if she was supposed to be someplace but couldn't quite remember where. Or maybe it was that she didn't feel well. It was an effort to talk.

Back on the second floor, she wandered over to a window seat and sat down. Being next to the casement window felt oddly comforting.

Calder was down on all fours looking up into the fireplace. "I'm just checking for hidden shelves. This building could be filled with secrets we haven't even imagined, you know?"

Hearing no response, he peered around at her. "What's the matter? You look like you're half asleep."

"Calder. These windows."

Calder sat up. "Yeah," he said slowly. "Kind of like Vermeer windows."

Petra looked around the room. "And the paneled wood. I mean, millions of old buildings have paneled wood, but these rectangles . . ." Petra's voice trailed off, and she stared at her reflection in the darkening glass.

Calder came over and sat down quietly next to her. "Do you want to look around some more?" he asked, sounding like his parents when they were trying to get him to do something but didn't want to be too obvious.

Petra looked steadily at him. "Calder. What are you thinking?"

"That you sound like we might be getting warm."

Petra was suddenly feeling horribly warm. "I might just be getting sick. Come on, let's get out of here."

They headed back to the first floor. They passed the weasels that became brass door handles, the carved flute player overhead, the stone lions mounted high above the landing. Petra, resting her hand on the railing as they walked slowly down the sweeping staircase, stopped with a jolt. Calder kept going.

The railings were a delicate tangle of iron grapevines and creatures. There were birds, mice, and lizards. Instead of newel posts at the bottom of the staircase, an intricately carved oak monkey clung to either end of the railing. *Monkey, panel, vines, flute, finds* . . . She could feel the blood beating wildly in her temples: *monkey, vines . . . monkey, vines . . . panel, flute, finds . . . FINDS!* Mrs. Sharpe's words: Petra stood frozen, one hand gripping the railing.

She saw Calder pawing obliviously through their soggy clothing for his jacket. She hoped her face wasn't revealing her wild, screaming thoughts. Walk, just walk normally. . . . A man looked up at her as she passed, putting down his paper. Was the world able to feel her heart pounding, her thoughts on fire? She grabbed her things and burst out the door into the merciful dusk.

"Petra? What's up?"

"Come on!"

Calder could hardly keep up with his friend as she half-ran, half-stumbled through the new snow. She hurried a block east on Fifty-ninth Street and glanced back. Calder looked back, too, suddenly frightened.

"Let's go home through backyards. We need to disappear, okay?"

Calder walked quickly next to Petra, their shoulders touching. He thought the P for *prey* — or was it *pray*? The blue shadows of late afternoon were menacing now. Bushes between houses seemed filled with pools of darkness, and people hunched against the cold looked dangerous.

When she was satisfied that they weren't being followed, Petra stopped. "Calder. This is it."

He looked around at the deserted alleyway and shivered. "This is *what*?"

"I think we've found her."

Chapter Twenty   A MANIAC

✖ ✖ ✖ As Petra brushed her teeth that night, she went over what had happened in Delia Dell Hall. There had been a clear *zap* in her mind. It reminded her of the time she'd been plugging a frayed lamp cord into the wall and her finger had landed on bare wire.

Had Mrs. Sharpe let something slip? Was she hoping they'd pick up on her clues? Petra thought of what Ms. Hussey had once said about criminals wanting to be discovered. If Mrs. Sharpe and Ms. Hussey had been collaborating —

And then, as if someone had changed the prescription on her glasses, she suddenly saw how wild her ideas had gotten. Were she and Calder crazy to think those two women could be mixed up in the theft? Their suspicions about their neighbor and their teacher suddenly seemed overwrought and childish. How could this staircase experience be anything but a huge, strange coincidence?

First of all, she and Calder and Mrs. Sharpe had been playing a game with pentominoes. Mrs. Sharpe obviously had never seen a pentomino before. The words she had made up that afternoon were not something she had planned.

Second, she was an old lady. She was the widow of a murder victim. She had gotten a letter from the thief. After weeks of worrying, she had turned it in. She had asked for police protection. And Ms. Hussey was a young teacher, and a dedicated one. Why would she ever get mixed up in a major art theft?

Petra tapped her toothbrush on the sink in a businesslike way. Her imagination had run away with her in Delia Dell. Hoping to get the mystery solved, she had jumped to some ridiculous conclusions. All this looking was making her crazy. The zap was probably from not feeling well, and Mrs. Sharpe's pentomino words were nothing more than a magnificent Charles Fort incident. The stolen painting was probably in Switzerland or Brazil or Japan. She'd apologize to Calder in the morning for scaring him.

In two days it would be her twelfth birthday. Twelve-year-olds were old enough to sort out what made sense and what didn't.

Petra put down her toothbrush and, sitting on the edge of the bathtub, waited for the water to get hot. She suddenly thought about the Lady. Am I thinking clearly? she wanted to ask her. Did I just imagine what happened today? Are you in Delia Dell? She waited for a response. There wasn't one.

Doubt seeped back into her mind. Since when had she been so rational? Imagining: that was what she was best at. And hadn't she and Calder agreed that they needed to rescue Ms. Hussey? And how about that letter she had just found in Mrs. Sharpe's bushes?

She hopped into the tub and put a hot washcloth on her head. Letting her neck flop backward, she closed her eyes.

Suddenly she found herself picturing a rectangle inside a triangle. It was more a feeling than an image. She dunked her head, letting the water run into her ears. Couldn't she stop thinking?

✖ ✖ ✖ It was a sparkling, whiter-than-white winter morning, a morning of brusque sky, inky black branches, and the blinding, two-dimensional look of new snow.

Glancing out her window as she dressed, Petra thought that the branches could be rivers on a map, or cracks on a blue plate. Maybe they were symbols in an unknown code — how do we know that trees don't talk deliberately with their branches, giving slow, intricate messages with an unnoticed vocabulary of shapes? Calder's thinking was infectious.

Whistling happily, Petra flew down the stairs to breakfast. The world felt rich with possibility. Her practical reasoning last night now seemed cowardly, unimaginative. What had gotten into her? She thought of the thief's phrase, *I congratulate you all on your pursuit of the truth.*

It was Saturday morning and her parents, still in pajamas, their heads almost touching, were absorbed in an article in the *Chicago Tribune.* They looked upset.

"The guy is a maniac! A self-absorbed lunatic!" Petra's father slammed his hand against the table. All the cereal bowls jumped.

"What's wrong?" Petra froze.

"More news on the Vermeer painting. We'll all have to pray that the FBI knows what they're doing." Frank Andalee stood up as he spoke, putting a hand on his daughter's shoulder. "Aren't you glad you aren't responsible for saving one of the world's masterpieces from a maniac?"

"Yeah, Dad." Her heart sinking, she began to read.

THE NATIONAL GALLERY OF ART RECEIVED THE FOLLOWING ANONYMOUS LETTER YESTERDAY. THE LAST COMMUNICATION FROM THE THIEF, AN ADVERTISEMENT SENT TO THE CHICAGO TRIBUNE, HAD BEEN MAILED FROM FLORENCE, ITALY. THE LETTER RECEIVED YESTERDAY WAS MAILED FROM A POST OFFICE IN WASHINGTON, D.C. BOTH THE FBI AND THE NATIONAL GALLERY OF ART FELT IT WAS IMPORTANT THAT THE PUBLIC KNOW IMMEDIATELY ABOUT THE THIEF'S LATEST INTENTIONS.

Dear National Gallery,
The recently released book, THE VERMEER DILEMMA: WHAT HAPPENS NOW? *points to the public's overwhelming response to my letter and the three advertisements I took out in newspapers around the world. They have, indeed, come to agree with me. Now it is up to you and to your colleagues to agree, publicly, with us all.*

I demand that you write letters to all other owners of Vermeer paintings. You are to state that my point of view is a valid one, and to request that the attributions that I identified earlier be changed immediately.

If these attributions are not changed within one month, by January 11, I will, against my desires, destroy A LADY WRITING. *I will consider it a sacrifice in the interest of truth, a lesson for those too rigid, too dishonest, to do what is right.*

I am old and will not live long. I will, however, live to see this resolved on museum walls and in writing or, to the horror of us all, in ashes.

I beg of you to spare A LADY WRITING. *If you look into your hearts, I know that you will, as I predicted in November, come to agree with me.*

Do what is right.

Petra dropped the paper and rushed out of the kitchen.

Chapter Twenty-one

✖ ✖ ✖ "This thief is way more ruthless than we thought." It was 9:00 A.M. and Calder and Petra were sitting in Calder's kitchen drinking hot chocolate. His parents were out grocery shopping.

"I'll bet if we called the police, Delia Dell would be searched today. And if the painting *is* there, they'd have a better chance of finding it than we would. The other thing we can do is tell our parents and leave it up to them." Petra didn't sound particularly happy about either idea.

Calder, absorbed in his own thoughts, grinned. "We can also tell no one. I can see the headlines now: 'Kids Locate Missing Vermeer' or 'Kids Brilliantly Track Down Vermeer Masterpiece' or 'Kids Lead Discouraged FBI Agents to —'"

"Calder! Come on! How can you even think about fame? What would be best for the Lady?" Petra closed her mouth in a tight, big-sister kind of line.

"To be found." Calder folded his arms across his chest and looked sulky. "You'd like to be on the news, too."

Petra paused to think about seeing herself on a talk show, or having her picture on the front of the *Chicago Tribune*. "Maybe," she said in a kinder voice.

"I vote we try to find it ourselves today, and if we don't, we talk to our parents and the police tonight."

"Fine. I think we should call Mrs. Sharpe first."

"Why?" Calder had pulled the I pentomino out of his pocket and was flipping it back and forth on the table. "Because the letter sounds like her talking? We know it's not. She's in the hospital and, besides, she would never harm a Vermeer."

"She might help us." Petra gave her mug a decisive tap with her spoon. "We'll tell her what happened in Delia Dell. That will make her curious. Then, if she knows something, maybe she'll just blurt it out."

Both were looking at the I. "What's it saying?" Petra asked.

"*Instant*," Calder said. "Guess that means 'get going.'"

They called the hospital and asked for Mrs. Sharpe's room.

When she answered, Petra said, "Calder and I were spending some time in Delia Dell yesterday —"

"And?" Mrs. Sharpe's voice could have cut steel.

"The letter in the paper . . . we're worried."

There was silence on the other end. "Mrs. Sharpe? We just didn't want you to worry. About us."

"Don't flatter yourselves. Why should I worry?"

Before Petra could tell her about the zap on the staircase, the old woman said, "Just be careful. Looking and seeing are two very different things."

The phone line went dead.

✖ ✖ ✖ Calder left his parents a note. He and Petra put on their coats and headed for the campus. They hurried in through the side door of Delia Dell, and Petra skidded on the wet floor tiles. Her feet went out from under her, and she came to a painful stop in front of one of the benches.

Scrambling to her knees, she looked up into a man's face. He had eyebrows so thick that they hung precariously over his eyes, which seemed far too small for the size of his face.

"Slippery stuff, is it not?" The man's voice was low and pleasant; he had a foreign accent. "Zees old floors are terrible vhen zey are vet. But it's a

vonderful building. Very vonderful." He smiled at Petra, his eyes almost vanishing beneath the outcroppings of hair. He offered her a large hand. "You two vere visiting ze ozzer day, no?" Something about this man was familiar.

Petra was on her feet. "I'm fine," she blurted, and shoved Calder back out the door in front of her.

"Great! That man noticed us, and you acted all nervous. *Now* what do we do?"

"What was I supposed to say, 'Which way to the Vermeer?' Did you recognize that voice? I think it was the man from the post office."

"What man?" Calder asked.

"The guy who stepped on Mrs. Sharpe's letter!"

"Well whoever he is, we could have just kept going. If we didn't stick out before, we sure do now."

This was the closest they had come to a fight. Petra's elbows were sore, and she was mad at herself. She knew Calder was right. After all, the man might be nobody.

"Wait," Calder said. "I have an idea. I think I remember a basement entrance."

They walked quickly around to the east side of

the rambling building. There, miraculously, was a small open door half a flight up behind a walled area. The door was propped open with a dented trash can.

"Wow! If anyone asks us what we're doing, we'll explain that we're making a plan of the building for school." Calder didn't sound as confident as he was trying to feel.

"Let's get out paper and pencils so it looks like we're really working on something," added Petra.

Armed with materials, they crept closer. It was hard to see into the darkened doorway. They paused outside, listening, then peered around the corner. There was no one in sight.

They tiptoed down a long corridor that curved to the left and then to the right. Swinging doors opened into a room with a single lightbulb overhead. Once inside, they were faced with three possible exits. They picked the one in the middle.

"*Ee-uw.*" Calder stepped over a nasty pile of garbage that smelled of sour milk and sneakers. Petra kept her mitten over her nose.

They were soon in a maze of small passageways.

"What direction do you suppose we're going

in?" Calder asked, looking around at the peeling paint.

"No idea, but I want it to be up," Petra said.

They found themselves at a fork. To their relief, one direction led to an iron stairwell. They hurried toward it.

On the second floor, a diamond-shaped window looked into a hall.

"I can't see much. You try." Calder stepped aside. At that moment a blue sweater flashed by. Both kids ducked, and Petra hit Calder in the nose with her hair clip.

"Pet-*ra*! Watch what you're doing, will you?" Calder forgot to whisper, and the sweater reappeared, pausing for several long seconds on the other side of the door before going on.

"Calder, that looked just like my dad's sweater. I've got to peek out."

"What'll we say if it is him? He'll ask what we're doing here."

"I don't know, but I need to see if that's my dad."

They went as quietly as they could down the hall past several offices. When they reached the corner, they saw the man in the blue sweater walking up the stairs to the third floor, carrying a smallish rectangular package.

The man was definitely Frank Andalee.

"Weird," Petra whispered. "What would he be doing here? He sometimes works Saturdays, but on the other side of campus."

Petra was remembering her dad's anger that morning, and the way he had pounded the table. She also remembered his words: *Aren't you glad you aren't responsible for saving one of the world's masterpieces from a maniac?* The word "maniac" echoed in a frightening way in her mind. Did he feel that *he* was responsible? Maybe he had stumbled onto something he shouldn't have and that was what had made him so grumpy lately.

She remembered him muttering the words "a loan," or had it been "alone"? Either one was spooky. And then there was the talk about two mysterious letters, and also what she'd overheard him saying that fall to her mom: *Everyone has something to hide.*

Seeing how miserable Petra looked, Calder patted her on the back. "I'm sure he has a good reason for being here."

Stashing backpacks and jackets in a window

seat, they began exploring the second floor of Delia Dell. During the next half hour they tapped, they studied, they pressed, they poked, they leaned, they tugged, they opened, they closed. Several closets appeared, walls creaked, but there was no sign of the painting.

Petra couldn't concentrate. "I just can't imagine what business he'd have in Delia Dell," she said.

"He'd be wondering the same thing if he saw you."

"And that package he was carrying was just the right size. . . ."

Petra suddenly felt very tired of suspecting people — first Mrs. Sharpe, then Ms. Hussey, then both of them, and now . . . her dad?

Calder seemed to pick up on her thoughts. "Sneaking around and trying to figure people out isn't as much fun as I thought it would be," he said.

Looking through one of the windows, she saw her dad and the man from the post office cross the parking lot.

"Calder! They're together!"

Petra noticed that her dad's shoulders were hunched and his hands were stuffed in his pockets. He was no longer carrying the package.

Chapter Twenty-two   TWELVES

✖ ✖ ✖ By the time Calder and Petra stepped outside, both men were gone. There were no footsteps to follow. The snow was packed into an unreadable mass.

"Guess we should go," Petra said.

"Yup."

On the way back to Harper Avenue, Calder and Petra made a plan. They would return to Delia Dell that night. Each would tell their parents that they were over at the other's house.

"I guess we may be headed for a life of crime after all." Petra gave Calder a halfhearted grin. "But this is different — it'll be an early birthday adventure. I mean —" She stopped short.

Now Calder looked uncomfortable. "How did you know?"

"How did I know what?"

"My birthday."

"What? It's my birthday, too!"

To Petra's surprise, Calder seemed more preoccupied than anything else.

He was looking at the T pentomino in his

right hand. "T for twelve. . . . We're both twelve on 12–12. . . . Why didn't I see this before?"

"Wow," was all Petra said.

He went on, "It's a puzzle that hinges on twelves. There are the pentominoes, of course, and the fact that we're both turning twelve on the twelfth day of the twelfth month, and I'll bet there's more about the painting or about Vermeer that works with twelves."

"Calder, you're either totally nuts or absolutely brilliant. Maybe both."

"And we have just about twelve hours to figure this out — think we can do it?"

"I do."

✖ ✖ ✖ That evening, the kids were crouched behind a bush just under the first-floor windows of Delia Dell. It was ten minutes to seven. The blue sky and white snow of the morning had deepened into an icy purple laced with black.

"It's the post office man!" whispered Calder. Sure enough, he was one of the last people to leave the building before the doors were locked. He walked slowly down the stairs to a parked car. Before he climbed in, he scanned Fifty-ninth Street as if checking for someone. Calder and Petra got a good look at his face.

As soon as his car was gone, Petra hopped out of the bush. "Quick!"

They hurried around the building to the garbage area. The back door they had entered that morning was still propped open.

They walked as fast as possible toward the dim opening and ducked inside. It felt like jumping into dark water.

They could hear footsteps several rooms away, and someone whistling.

Petra grabbed Calder's sleeve and pointed to a giant file cabinet. They crouched next to it, hardly daring to breathe.

The footsteps came closer, quick and heavy, and there was a grunt as someone put down a metal trash can. Both could see a man moving around in the shadows.

Another two steps and he was slamming the back door, locking it with a double bolt. He switched off the light from the next room, leaving them in darkness. The footsteps grew fainter. They waited until they heard another door shut.

Petra pulled the flashlight out of her backpack. It went on and then off. She shook it vigorously. Nothing happened. She felt the darkness clamping down on them, and heard a noise like the ocean in her ears. The space around them started to shrink in an extremely unfriendly way.

"Oh, great!"

"Didn't you test it at home?"

"Of course I did!"

To their relief, the light came back on. Petra kept it pointed toward the ceiling.

Carrying the flashlight like a full glass of water, they walked carefully through the shadowy maze of halls and storage rooms. Nothing looked familiar. They must have taken a different turn. Calder was thinking to himself that "spooky" would be a mild word for this place. It made the basement in Gracie feel cozy.

Both tried not to think about anything but the next step.

The passageways felt endless. The flashlight went out once more, and this time stayed out. Holding on to each other, they groped their way around the next corner.

A red exit sign glowed in the distance.

"We did it!" They made their way down the corridor and finally through the door. They found themselves standing in the big entrance hall.

A high-backed choir bench in the center of the room towered above them. The moon had risen since they'd been outside, and light came through the casement windows on the second-floor landing. A path of broken rectangles and rhombi spilled crazily down the stairs, coming to rest on the heads of the wooden monkeys at the base.

"Maybe it's good the flashlight's out, in case someone is watching the building," Petra whispered.

"I was thinking the same thing." Calder glanced toward the banquet room and library.

Feeling small in the darkness, they walked through the entrance hall and up several steps to the next room. They headed under the arbor of plaster grapes and into the library.

The room was cavernous and lonely at night. Outside, students wandering back to their dormitories were talking and laughing. Petra and Calder felt separated from everyday life by a chasm of responsibility. What had ever made them think they could do this?

"Let's start over here, and stay together," Petra said. Looking for concealed closets or panels or knobs, they tapped along the south wall, straining their eyes against the shadows. It was slow-going.

They hesitated at the door to the dining room, peering into deeper darkness. There weren't as many windows here. Once in, they worked methodically, moving faster now. They pressed and knocked so hard on every panel that their arms were trembling and their knuckles raw.

Calder turned, moving so quickly that Petra jumped back. "What?"

No answer. Calder was running toward the stairs.

Petra raced after him. "Calder! Wait up!"

He stopped at the bottom of the stairs and walked up twelve steps, counting as he went. "What is it?" Petra's voice was a squeak.

"I think I've figured it out. Go back down."

"By *myself*?"

"Hurry! Stay right under the twelfth step." Calder was breathless but calm.

Petra thought she could see figures crouched in

every corner. If she disappeared like Frog, it would be all Calder's fault.

"Here?" Petra's heart was pounding. It was painfully dark by the side of the staircase. Suddenly she remembered her thought in the bathtub: a rectangle inside a triangle. She was standing against a huge triangle.

"One step farther." Calder rushed down and crouched next to her. He ran his fingers over the surface of the wall. It was covered with small square panels, each about four inches wide.

"A series of twelves," Calder was muttering. ". . . six, seven, eight . . . here."

They tried rapping on the twelfth rectangle and then on the ones around it. There was clearly space behind this section of the wall.

They leaned with all their strength against the carved oak. Nothing happened.

"Let's press more slowly. Maybe there's a spring or a latch." Petra started on the upper right and Calder on the upper left. They worked their way carefully down for several inches.

They did this twice, each time trying to center the twelfth panel in a larger, imaginary rectangle. The third time, something gave.

There was a splintery groan and a loud thump. The panel slid back into the wall, revealing a shallow storage area.

Petra, trembling now, felt automatically for the flashlight and fumbled with the switch. Miraculously, it turned on.

"Oh my God, Petra!"

Leaning against the back wall, wrapped in a cloth covering, was a smallish rectangular shape.

Calder took a shaky step backward. Handing the flashlight to him, Petra lifted out the object. The wrapping was velvet.

Side by side, they sank down onto the floor. Petra began to unwind the fabric, turning the object first one way and then the other, yards of deep red falling in folds around her knees. She touched the corner of a frame. The wood was cool and smooth. She stopped moving.

"You." The word was barely a sound.

Calder understood and carefully lifted the last layer of velvet.

It was a moment they would remember with perfect clarity for the rest of their lives. The flashlight picked up an answering glimmer from the pearls, from the satiny hair ribbons,

from the woman's eyes: The image was finer and more delicate than either of them had imagined. Hot tears began running down Petra's cheeks, blurring her vision of the woman's familiar face.

Hearing a stifled sob, Calder felt his eyes suddenly fill. At that moment, there were just the three of them in the world: the Lady, who was almost 350 years old, and the two children, who were almost twelve.

"We'll get you out of here," Petra whispered, not trusting her voice.

Calder, wiping his cheeks on the sleeve of his jacket, pointed to the strand of pearls lying on the table. "Count."

Petra did. She looked shyly at Calder, aware that they'd both been crying. "Ten? Oh I don't believe it! The pearl earrings make twelve!"

They gave each other a wobbly smile.

"What made you see that?" Petra asked.

"I don't know. Maybe she did."

Petra, still looking at the painting, nodded in silent understanding.

There was a clearing of throats. They hadn't thought about what to do if they actually found her.

"Calder, it's so cold out. Do you suppose it will hurt her? I could wrap her in my jacket."

"We'll have to. It'd be worse to leave her. What if the thief decided to move her tomorrow? We'd never forgive ourselves."

As Calder held the flashlight, Petra rewrapped the painting carefully in the long strip of velvet, and then took off her sweater and tied it securely around the bundle. The wide frame made it an awkward size to carry.

They walked across the dark entrance hall, both hardly feeling the tiles under their feet, and headed for one of the exits on the north side of the building.

Scanning the edges of the door, they spotted the telltale red light of an alarm.

"I'll bet all of these main doors are wired," Calder said. "We could try to get out through the basement, but that may be wired also. Or you could run from here and I could distract anyone who saw us."

"No. Let's stick together."

"Maybe I should be carrying something, too, just in case someone is watching the building. It doesn't matter if the police pick us up, right? In fact, that would be a relief."

Calder reached down and grabbed a DANGER: SLIPPERY WHEN WET sign that had been left by the door and padded it with a stack of university newspapers. He quickly pulled off his jacket, wrapped the papers and sign tightly in his sweatshirt, and put his jacket back on. He held the bundle in front of him as if it were fragile.

"Convincing? Wait." Calder reached into his pocket and pulled out a pentomino. "It's Y for *yes*. We're going to get her home." He tapped it gently on Petra's package.

"Absolutely." Petra was smiling now.

"Ready?" Both took a deep and shaky breath.

"On our marks —"

"Get set —"

"Go!"

They opened the door and started running into the cold night air, the alarm screaming behind them.

Chapter Twenty-three HELP!

✖ ✖ ✖ Petra and Calder raced toward the garden and playground behind the U. School. They looked back every few seconds. A man in a dark jacket appeared from around the Fifty-ninth Street side of the building. He was running in their direction.

"Can you see who it is?" Petra's voice was jagged.

"Are you the police?" yelled Calder.

There was no answer. Gasping for air, they paused for just a second, ready to hug a university policeman. At that moment the figure emerged from shadow and the moon caught the flat planes of his glasses, turning his eyes into pools of silver. He was moving directly toward them, and moving as if his life depended on it. He was not in uniform.

"Run!" Calder panted. Both kids took off, zigzagging around trees and bushes.

"HELP! HELP!" shrieked Petra. There was no one ahead of them. Where were the dog walkers, the students?

The man was gaining on them. They could now hear his breathing. Petra leaped over a sand box and headed out of the playground. She heard a *thud* just behind her, and out of the corner of her eye she saw Calder falling over the edge of the climbing equipment.

She stopped.

Calder shouted, "Go! GO!" He was up again, but the man was mere seconds behind him now.

Petra ran as she had never run before. She looked back to see Calder high on top of the slide, still clutching his bundle, the man standing below.

She could hear Calder's voice piercingly high with fright: "If you come any closer, I'll put my knee through it. I will. Then you'll be in big trouble." She couldn't understand the man's growly reply. Calder's voice drifted back: "You wouldn't dare hurt me!" She felt a sharp flash of fear for Calder, and at the same moment a flood of admiration for his quick thinking and bravery.

She was on Fifty-seventh Street now. She raced down the block to the Medici Restaurant, pulled open the heavy wooden door, and flung herself inside.

Luckily, a member of the university police was just leaving. Petra panted out her story about Calder and a man in the playground. She decided

not to say anything about the Lady. She didn't want to waste time on questions. They hurried to the alleyway, and she jumped into the front seat of the policeman's car. Minutes later, they pulled up next to the playground.

The blue lights swept across a form on the ground. She heard the policeman grunt, then say, "Stay where you are, kid," as he reached for his door handle. Leaving the painting on the front seat, Petra leaped out anyway.

As they got closer to the slide, she saw that the lump was Calder's sweatshirt on top of a flurry of newspapers, the papers he'd carried when they'd run from Delia Dell. "Oh yes! Calder got away!" Petra hopped up and down.

The policeman knelt to look at the sweatshirt. "Looks like there's blood on it," he said.

Horrified, Petra knelt, too. She saw drips of dark liquid on the gray hood.

"Come on, kid — you shouldn't be over here." The policeman stood up. Then he shouted, "You! Stop right now! This is the police!"

Petra looked up to see the man who had chased them duck out of the patrol car. Her bundle was tucked under his arm. He ran east on Fifty-eighth Street, toward the yards and fences that Petra knew could hide him.

"That's him! That's the guy who was chasing us, and now he's stolen the painting!"

"He's got *what?*"

"Oh, please hurry!"

The policeman, one hand on his holster, ran to the patrol car. "Assault suspect heading east on Fifty-eighth Street — carrying stolen item. Immediate help requested."

"Say it's priceless, it's the Vermeer!"

Hesitating a moment, the policeman said gently, "Honey, they'll be right here."

"I'm telling you the TRUTH!"

Again, the policeman looked at her indulgently and shook his head. "What were you two doing out here alone at this hour, anyway?"

Petra whispered, "You wouldn't understand if I told you. Oh I hope Calder is all right!"

Petra, crying now, could hardly give her friend's address and telephone number. She had failed him and failed the Lady, and now Calder was hurt.

As they headed for the police station, she said in a still-shaky voice, "If you've ever believed in anything, please believe me now."

✖ ✖ ✖ Calder was reported as missing. His parents and Petra's parents set off immediately to search the neighborhood with the police. The Pillays and Andalees were shocked and excited by Petra's news, but there was no time for explanations. Calder's disappearance was more than a little frightening.

A neighbor stayed in the Pillays' house in case Calder got back on his own. Down the street, Petra was left home with the younger kids, who were all asleep. Still dressed, she paced back and forth in her front hall. Where would Calder have gone? And how did he get away from that man who ran so fast?

She sat down on the front stairs. What if the man hurt Calder in the playground and then dragged him off someplace? She tried not to picture it. Stay positive, she said to herself. Calder would never let that happen.

She asked herself where she would leave the painting if she were the thief and were trying to escape from Hyde Park unnoticed. At least she could think about that.

She imagined the Lady, wrapped in velvet

under her sweater. Show me where you are, Petra thought. Please help me find you. Suddenly she felt, she *knew*, the Lady was close by. Could the thief have stuck her underneath someone's porch? In a recycling bin, or a clump of bushes? No, he wouldn't be stupid enough to endanger her. She thought of a garage, but they were usually locked. Then she had another idea.

Petra grabbed a snow shovel from her front hall and headed out to the sidewalk. Her brothers and sisters wouldn't wake up, and besides, this would only take a couple of minutes. She'd be careful.

The Castiglione's tree house was right next door. Their kids were grown, and it was rarely used anymore. Petra thought she'd just take a look and see if anyone had left prints beneath it in the snow. If so, she'd go back in and call the police.

She shut the front door quietly behind her. There was a patrol car at the end of the block, moving in the opposite direction, the sound of the engine fading away. Silence. The moon was full and bright.

Stepping into the Castiglione's backyard, she held the snow shovel across her body like a weapon. And then she saw the boot prints ending in a trampled place under the tree. They were the size of a man's feet.

She stood for a moment, listening and looking up at the tree house. If those prints belonged to the thief, could he still be up there? It had been more than an hour since he'd grabbed the painting from the patrol car. Why would he sit up there in the cold, waiting for someone to find him?

There was only one set of prints, but Petra knew from experience that it was possible to leave the tree house by inching along a big branch and dropping down on the high bank near the train tracks. He could have hidden the Lady and gotten on a train or a bus unnoticed.

The tree house was a small structure with one glass window. It was more or less weatherproof, so it could work as a safe hiding place. She made a snowball and heaved it at the house. It thumped lightly on the side. She threw several more. If someone was in there, she hoped he'd look out and she could run.

Nothing.

"You up there!" she called in a shaky voice.

No response.

Petra had to do it. Propping the shovel against the tree, she began to climb.

One foot, one hand, next foot, other hand . . . Petra counted as she climbed. As she grabbed the twelfth board, she tried to steady the pounding in her throat. She was now just under the trapdoor. She paused, breathing deeply and listening. Her pulse seemed to be whispering, *twelve, twelve, twelve, twelve.*

She pushed gently on the trapdoor. No sound from inside. No big hand slammed it closed or jerked it open.

She pushed harder. The door fell back with a *thud*.

She stepped up onto the next rung and peered into the house.

"Calder!" she gasped.

He was lying on his side, curled into a U shape around the bundle. She shook him by the shoulder. She grabbed one hand and patted it and rubbed it. It was icy cold.

"Oh, Calder! What happened to you?"

His eyes opened and closed. "Knocked me off the slide . . . head hurts . . . but I followed him. . . ."

"That's okay, don't talk. We're almost safe now — you, me, and the Lady," Petra said soothingly. She took off her jacket, wrapped Calder in it, and started quickly down the ladder to get help.

"You'll never guess," Calder muttered.

Chapter Twenty-four   THE PIECES

✖ ✖ ✖ Old Fred had been found dead on the train in the early hours of the morning, having suffered a massive heart attack. He was wearing boots that matched the prints around the base of the Castiglione's tree house.

Although Fred's beard was gone and his glasses were different, Calder had recognized his voice. Fred had knocked him off the slide, and Calder had hit his head in the fall. He then pretended to be unconscious. When it looked like Fred was gone, Calder got to his feet. His head was pounding, he was dizzy, and there was no sign of Petra. He hoped with all his heart that she had gotten help before Fred caught up with her.

Calder started for home, moving unsteadily through backyards. He was just resting in the bushes when Fred ran by carrying the Lady. Calder followed. Hiding behind bushes he watched Fred climb up to the Castiglione's tree house with the painting. When he heard the loud crack of a tree branch and saw Fred scramble up onto the tracks, he felt there was no time to go get official help. He had to get the Lady down. Fred might be sending someone back within minutes to retrieve her.

Calder staggered across the Castiglione's backyard, tried to step carefully in Fred's footprints so as not to leave a trail, and climbed the tree. When he reached the platform and saw that the painting was safe, he stopped to rest. That was when he passed out. Shortly after, Petra found him, possibly saving his life. He had a nasty concussion, but recovered enough to have birthday cake the next day with his friend. Petra reminded him that they were now even. He had probably saved her life by distracting Old Fred while she ran with the painting.

✖ ✖ ✖ Fred Steadman's name, it turned out, was Xavier Glitts. He was the leader of an international crime ring. The FBI discovered that Glitts had advanced degrees from the Sorbonne in Paris and from Princeton University. His nickname, in the world of art theft, was "Glitter Man." He was famous for changing identities and for charming his way in and out of impossible situations.

In addition to his New York home, he had an apartment in London, and one in Rome. All of his files on the theft of *A Lady Writing* turned up in a bank vault in Switzerland.

Xavier Glitts had a customer who had wanted for many years to own this particular Vermeer masterpiece. The collector, a clever criminal himself, would pay Glitts sixty million dollars for her, but wanted a guarantee that the police would never trace the theft.

Glitter Man had come up with what he'd thought was a brilliant plan. He would pose as an idealistic thief. He picked Hyde Park as the perfect community in which to hide, and the role of Zelda Segovia's husband as a perfect disguise.

Shortly after he and Zelda were married, they attended a fund-raising dinner at the University School. There he chatted with a young teacher named Isabel Hussey who had just been hired to teach at the school in the fall. Discovering that she had been trained as an art historian, he drew her into a discussion about Vermeer, pretending to be ignorant himself about the painter's work. Ms. Hussey gave him all the ideas about attribution that went into the thief's letters.

At the University of Chicago's archives, Xavier Glitts gained the trust of one of the research librarians, who told him about a secret compartment in Delia Dell Hall, a compartment that was supposedly under the main staircase. Glitts had explained to the librarian that he was documenting "secret storage places" in the greatest universities in the world, and claimed that he had heard of several at Oxford, at Harvard, at McGill, and at the University of Salamanca. The librarian at the University of Chicago was happy to tell him all she knew.

While living on Harper Avenue, Glitts heard about his reclusive neighbor Louise Sharpe, and soon found out she was Leland Sharpe's widow. She, like Ms. Hussey, had passionate feelings about Vermeer's work. It was almost too good to be true.

And then Glitts met Vincent Watch at Powell's. They chatted, and Mr. Watch mentioned that his two great loves were art books and mysteries, and that he hoped one day to write an art mystery that focused on real issues in the art world. He had never gotten around to writing such a book, but had dreamed about it for years. Glitts had nodded sympathetically.

According to a journal found by the FBI in Glitts's bank vault, he came up with the idea of the three letters in order to confuse the authorities and to create three suspects. Then he had fun writing the letters that were published by newspapers, and watching the public's reaction. His theft had become a one-of-a-kind world event, and he was a hero to thousands of people. He was only sorry that no one would ever know he was responsible.

After writing the letter in which he threatened to burn the painting, and in which he said he was "old and would not live long" — hoping, obviously, to sound like Mrs. Sharpe — Glitts had planned to remove *A Lady Writing* from the secret compartment, deliver it for his sixty million dollars, and allow the world to believe it had been burned. He was quite sure that no museum would meet the demands in his last letter.

The FBI speculated that on the night he returned to Delia Dell Hall to get the painting, he had just parked his car when he heard the building alarm go off, and then saw Calder and Petra running. That was where things started to go wrong.

✖ ✖ ✖ In their investigations, the FBI found that Mrs. Sharpe had a great deal of money and that she had made a very generous gift to the National Gallery *after* the theft had taken place. She explained in a steely tone that she had wanted to remain anonymous, disliking publicity after the circumstances of her husband's death. She had intended the money to pay for gatherings of Vermeer scholars to work on attribution and on the crime. When the money was used to pay for *The Vermeer Dilemma,* she was surprised but could hardly complain, given her request.

✖ ✖ ✖ Ms. Hussey was horrified when she heard from Mrs. Sharpe about everything Calder and Petra had done to protect her. Never having lived in a big city, she had been lonely and home-sick that fall. She had received a strange letter. When the painting was stolen and she realized that her ideas about Vermeer's work sounded like the thief's, she had been frightened. Trying to fig-ure out what to do with the thief's letter had been the final straw. She had no one to talk to in Chicago — no one, that is, but her sixth-grade class.

✖ ✖ ✖ Zelda Segovia was horrified that she'd been charmed into marrying a professional criminal. She knew nothing about Xavier Glitts or his shady business. When Tommy found out that his stepfather's real nickname was Glitter Man, he snorted. "More like Twitter Man. I never heard so much gabbing in my life. The way he promised stuff and then figured out how to take it away — what a sneak."

✖ ✖ ✖ Frank Andalee felt terrible about having frightened Petra that day in Delia Dell Hall. He had been delivering an old print from one of the science labs to the guy with the big eyebrows, who was a publicity man working for the university. Petra's dad changed departments that winter and was much happier with his new job.

✖ ✖ ✖ Vincent Watch had carried the letter around with him for weeks, getting a secret thrill from knowing it was in his pocket. He didn't want to contact the police before he was sure the thief wasn't going to contact him with an interesting proposal that he could then use in a book. The letter would be a good way to begin an art mystery. When the news came out about Mrs. Sharpe and Ms. Hussey being the other two recipients, he decided to confide in Mrs. Sharpe. He knew she wouldn't talk and would give him sound advice about whether to call the police.

After Calder's last delivery to Mrs. Sharpe, Mr. Watch stopped by her house on the way home from work. When he reached into his pocket to show Mrs. Sharpe the letter, it was gone. He never understood how this had happened. He must have missed his pocket the last time he slid the letter back in, and it must have fallen out on his walk down Harper Avenue. He was extremely upset, but Mrs. Sharpe was sympathetic and practical. They agreed that it no longer made sense for him to tell the authorities about the third letter. Since he had no proof of having gotten it, he'd just look silly.

This, strangely, was the second time he'd lost the letter. He'd made a copy weeks earlier, in case he lost the original, and it had somehow gotten away from him between the copy store and Powell's. It was almost eerie.

This was the letter Petra saw blowing around, but as Mr. Watch hadn't told Mrs. Sharpe about it, Petra never knew where it came from. She told Mrs. Sharpe about finding the third letter tucked neatly into the bushes. They agreed it was a chain of events that would have intrigued Charles Fort.

✖ ✖ ✖ As soon as the FBI had finished their questioning, Mrs. Sharpe, Calder, and Petra got together again for tea in Mrs. Sharpe's kitchen. This time, the tulips were yellow.

Mrs. Sharpe congratulated the children on their extraordinary bravery and intelligence. Coming from her, this was quite a compliment. After tea, Calder filled in Mrs. Sharpe on all the patterns of twelve he had identified. He told her about his pentominoes seeming to give him messages. He explained that he was quite sure there were more twelves involved.

Mrs. Sharpe's eyes became slits, as they had in the hospital when Petra had talked about her dream. The old woman was very quiet. They told her about the *"monkey-panel-vines-flute-finds"* moment on the stairs in Delia Dell. They asked her if she had done that on purpose.

"I wish," she said, giving them a smile that was almost wistful.

She thanked them both for sharing such

fabulous secrets and promised she would never tell those secrets to another soul — not without their permission. Somehow, Calder and Petra knew they could trust her.

Then she offered a secret of her own, and asked them to keep it until after her death. Both agreed immediately, and Petra reached out to pat Mrs. Sharpe's bony hand.

Mrs. Sharpe went over some of what Calder and Petra had already heard about her past. She said that just before her husband, Leland, had been murdered, she had received a letter from him saying he had made a stunning discovery about Vermeer's paintings, a discovery that would shake art historians all over the world. He couldn't wait to tell her about it, but wanted to save the news until he was "safe and sound in Hyde Park." And then, on the day he was due to fly back to Chicago, his body was found outside the Rijksmuseum in Amsterdam. He had been killed by a blow to the head. His date book had been in his suitcase, which was in the hotel lobby. When Mrs. Sharpe looked in the date book weeks later, she saw *1212* scribbled hurriedly, in his handwriting, on the day of his death. She pointed this out to the police, but no one knew what to make of it. Did it mean twelve minutes past noon, or past midnight? Did it represent the number 1,212? She wasn't able to figure it out, either. The police never brought anyone to trial, and the mystery had faded over time.

After telling the children this story, Mrs. Sharpe sat quietly for a moment, looking down at the table. Then she blinked rapidly, sat up straight, and blew her nose.

She continued in her familiar businesslike tone. "I became determined to pick up where Leland had left off, but I never could figure out exactly what it was he had uncovered or realized. In the years since, I've studied everything I could about Vermeer. I vowed that I would support any new research on his life or his paintings. And then, last fall, something very odd began to happen to me. And this is the part I want you to keep a secret."

Mrs. Sharpe said she had been "told" by the woman in *A Lady Writing* to clear the name of Vermeer, to make sure that the world knew that a number of his works had been done by followers. She had received pages and pages of messages, words she said she had merely written down. Calder and Petra looked at each other as Mrs. Sharpe disappeared to get a sheet of paper from the pile next to her computer. She settled back down at the kitchen table. This is what she read:

My lie is that I am only canvas and pigment. My truth is that I am alive. Some might call this your imagination, but it's not. Art, as you know, is about ideas. I am as real as your blue china or the boy with the box or the girl who dreamed about me. I am very much here.

Seeing how sober the children's faces had become, Mrs. Sharpe stopped to reassure them. "I am sharing this with you just to show you what I am beginning to see: Something much more powerful than any one of us has pulled us all together. Although Xavier Glitts thought he was in control, he was just a piece of the picture, if you'll pardon the pun. Something managed to communicate with each of us, including the thief, each in a way that we were willing to hear or see."

With the flicker of a smile, Mrs. Sharpe reached across the wooden table to straighten a tulip. Catching the afternoon sun, the petals filled with color, a clean cup of lemon in the winter light. Suddenly Petra remembered picking up a leaf on Harper Avenue that fall, and being struck by the thought that yellow was the color of surprise.

✖ ✖ ✖ Calder did discover more twelves. First he made a list:

Petra Andalee

Frank Andalee

Norma Andalee

Calder Pillay

Walter Pillay

Yvette Pillay

Isabel Hussey

Louise Sharpe

Tommy Segovia

Zelda Segovia

Vincent Watch

Xavier Glitts (also known as Fred Steadman)

There were twelve names, and twelve letters in each name. Mrs. Sharpe got all pink-cheeked and pleased when Calder showed her the list, and after thinking for a moment, she said slowly, "Yes, how curious . . . the message '1212' also has twelve letters if you spell it out, and so does the name of the painting, *A Lady Writing,* at least in English." She reminded Calder and Petra that Charles Fort didn't believe in coincidence. He felt things were often connected in ways that no one could yet explain in scientific terms. But if none of this was coincidence, what was it?

Calder and Petra were more than a little spooked by it all. They were very glad that they had Mrs. Sharpe to talk to. They thought it was pretty extraordinary that she had, in the hospital, said just about the same thing as Picasso about art, lies, and the truth. Maybe the greatest ideas were quite simple. Or maybe certain experiences in life were made to fit together like pentominoes. Maybe the passage of time, even centuries, didn't matter when something really important needed to be said.

If there were twelve names involved, and if each name was a piece in a very big puzzle, did any of those twelve fit together in other ways? Over many cups of tea, Calder, Petra, and Mrs. Sharpe found a number of odd connections.

The most startling one was that the first letter of the first name of each person on Calder's list was a pentomino. "The U is my C," Calder explained. "It's just a matter of a simple turn, not even a flip. I never liked the U being a U, anyway."

Calder then realized that if you thought about those twelve people as pentominoes, you could see that certain ones fit into rectangles more easily than others. The X (Xavier), for instance, is the hardest pentomino to work with. The U or C (Calder) and the P (Petra), however, work easily into many solutions. The L (Louise) can fit easily with the I (Isabel), and the W (Walter) with the Y (Yvette), or the F (Frank) with the N (Norma). . . . Calder's thoughts were running wild. Then he and Petra remembered Ms. Hussey saying *The letter is dead* at the beginning of the school year. Well, one letter certainly was, they thought grimly: the X.

Although Leland Sharpe was not on the list, Calder noticed that the first letter of his first name began with the twelfth letter in the alphabet. Petra added that L was a very useful pentomino and worked easily into most rectangles. "Yes, he always did manage to fit into every new situation."

Mrs. Sharpe sniffed and looked pleased. "He loved puzzles and codes, you know. He would have appreciated pentominoes."

Isabel Hussey and Louise Sharpe both turned out to be descendants of a member of the Coffin family on Nantucket Island. Both had lived there. Mrs. Sharpe *had* written the letter she'd told Calder and Petra about.

After the mystery was solved, Ms. Hussey and Mrs. Sharpe were often seen having dinner together in Hyde Park. They had lots to talk about and enjoyed each other's thinking. As the school year went on, Ms. Hussey became as much a friend as a teacher to Petra and Calder. The three often went to Fargo Hall after school for hot chocolate.

Petra did show Ms. Hussey her copy of *Lo!* The sixth-grade class tried to add to Charles Fort's accounts and studied the idea of coincidence. Was it, as a number of interested scientists believed, just the human fascination with patterns? Or was it something more?

Frank and Norma Andalee and Walter and Yvette Pillay all turned out to be forty-three years old. They had all been twelve in the year of Leland

Sharpe's death, which had been thirty-one years earlier. Mrs. Sharpe and the children wondered if there was any connection with the 1931 publication date of *Lo!* They also realized, with a shudder, that Vermeer had been forty-three when he died.

Petra's dad told Petra something else stunning: A part of his family had lived for centuries in the Netherlands, in an area not far from Delft. Family records were sketchy, but it was entirely possible that Petra was related to a member of Vermeer's family. Petra walked on air for days.

Calder, in his research, found that Johannes Vermeer had collapsed, quite suddenly, in December 1675. He had been buried in the Oude Kerk, in Delft, on December 16. It was thought that he died several days earlier, which would have made December 12 perhaps the last full day of his life. In addition to being Petra's and Calder's birthday, it had also been the last conscious day of Xavier Glitts's life.

And then there was Frog. Once Petra remembered Fort's sentence *We shall pick up an existence by its frogs*, she pointed out to Calder that perhaps it had been some kind of strange clue.

Maybe they should have picked up Glitter Man's existence from Frog.

Within weeks of the Lady's return to the National Gallery, the wall labels on a number of Vermeer paintings around the world were quietly changed to: ATTRIBUTED TO JOHANNES VERMEER. In celebration, Calder and Petra went to the Drake Hotel with Mrs. Sharpe for tea, and she told them both about deliveries that were soon to be made at each of their houses. She gave Calder an antique globe and a real Oriental carpet that looked just like the Geographer's. She gave her writing desk, an elegant seventeenth-century beauty, to Petra. She also gave her a string of real Dutch pearls.

Calder and Petra, in their interviews with the press, didn't share the entire story. They never mentioned Petra's dream, Calder's problem-solving, Charles Fort, the twelves, or the blue ones. They didn't know if the world was ready for it. And they still weren't entirely sure what had been real and what had not.

AFTER WORDS™

BLUE BALLIETT'S

Chasing Vermeer

ILLUSTRATED BY BRETT HELQUIST

CONTENTS

After Words™ guide by Leslie Budnick

About the Author

Blue Balliett was born in New York City and grew up playing in Central Park with her sister and brother and riding the public buses and subways. She lived on the sixth floor of an apartment building and played ball and rollerskated on the sidewalk outside. Some of her favorite memories of the city include the dizzying cherry blossoms around the reservoir on 90th Street and 5th Avenue in Central Park, and coconut Good Humor ice cream bars (no longer made!) from the truck outside the Guggenheim Museum.

After graduating from Brown University with an art history degree, Blue moved out to Nantucket Island — a tiny island just off the coast of Massachusetts — in order to write. There, Blue followed another interest — unexplainable events — and wrote two books of ghost stories, which she collected by interviewing people who lived on Nantucket Island. During that time she worked as a grill cook, a waitress, a researcher of old houses, and an art gallery director. That's also when she met and married her husband and had two children. As a family they spent as much time as possible on or in the water.

When her kids started school the family moved to Chicago, to the neighborhood known as Hyde Park (sound familiar?). Blue began teaching third grade at the University of Chicago Laboratory Schools. One year she and her class decided to figure out what art was about. They were looking for ways to feel comfortable thinking about art and the real questions art historians live with. They made countless discoveries, visited many museums in the city, and had scavenger hunts that resulted in setting off a number of alarms — by mistake, of course.

While these experiences were part of the inspiration behind *Chasing Vermeer*, Blue also wrote the book to explore the ways in which people perceive connections between supposedly unrelated events and situations, connections that many people miss. Is a coincidence just a coincidence?

It took Blue five years to finish *Chasing Vermeer*, as she was also teaching full-time. She says writing the book was like weaving: She did the warp based on art, wove across that with the pentominoes, and added in the classroom scenes. Now she's writing full-time, assisted by the family's twenty-pound cat, who helps by lying on the manuscript, shuffling pages, burying pencils under his belly, and generally keeping things mysterious.

About the Illustrator

Brett Helquist was born in a small town in Arizona where there was nothing to see for miles around, except a lot of red dirt. With not much for him or his six sisters to do, he learned to use his imagination. That and his discovery of the newspaper comic strips — his favorite was "Alley Oop"— started him off drawing. He dreamed of one day creating his own comic strips.

When Brett was about eleven years old, his family moved to Utah, where there was a lot to do. He became interested in fishing, hiking, and camping, and didn't think very much about being an artist anymore. He decided he wanted to be a scientist in order to better understand the world around him.

Then while Brett was in college at Brigham Young University, he started to think about art again. He began as an engineering major but soon realized that was not the right choice, so he decided to take some time off and headed for Taiwan. There he stumbled into work illustrating textbooks and a year later went back to school as an illustration major. From that moment on, he knew what he wanted to do.

Soon after graduation he moved to New York City, where he has remained with his wife for the past ten years. Before becoming a full-time illustrator, Brett worked as a graphic designer. His illustrations have appeared in magazines, newspapers, picture books, and novels. As an artist Brett tries to be observant, to look carefully, and to discover the beautiful and amazing things all around him.

Q&A with Blue Balliett

Q: *What was it like for you growing up in New York City?*
A: Growing up in New York City was both hard and exciting, because the noise and the action never stop. I was allowed to go around the city on my own when I was quite young, and I loved that freedom, but I sometimes got tired of all the concrete and people. Maybe that's part of the reason I liked New York's museums so much — when I was growing up, they were easy to duck in and out of, and a peaceful place to think or hang out.

Q: *Is Vermeer your favorite painter?*
A: There are many painters I admire, but Vermeer is certainly one of my favorites. Eight of the thirty-five paintings attributed to him are in New York City, so I first saw his work a long time ago. I remember associating him with a cozy, orderly yet mysterious world. The people in his paintings all looked kind to me.

Q: *Ms. Hussey encourages her students to think for themselves and ask questions without worrying about limitations or rules. You were a teacher for over ten years. What were some unusual assignments you gave your students?*
A: Some assignments included turning yourself into an architectural detail on a building and writing about it; making a scale drawing of your home and recording each family member's favorite spot, then interviewing each person about that choice; sitting in front of a window for an hour and recording what you see in as much detail as possible and then using one detail to begin a mystery story. I could go on and on — each

year I tried to build on the interests and curiosities of that particular class, so we did many kinds of investigations.

Q: *How did you come up with the names Calder and Petra? Do they have specific origins and significance?*

A: Calder's name comes from Alexander Calder, who was a modern artist with a giant sunburst of a spirit — I've always loved his work and his ideas. Petra's name came from an article in *National Geographic* magazine that I stumbled on when I was cleaning off the coffee table at home. I have always enjoyed having an unusual name, and I wanted to give Calder and Petra distinctive names also. Although Elizabeth is the name on my birth certificate, I've been called Blue — after the color of a deep, clear sky — all my life.

Q: *Calder and Petra try to see situations in a different light and to question what they think they know. Do you try to do the same in your day-to-day life?*

A: Yes, I do. I've found that if you question the way in which you're seeing something familiar, you almost always catch an unexpected idea or detail. Sometimes you uncover big surprises. I also think that if you look at almost anything closely enough, it becomes intriguing.

Q: *Do you keep a journal of unexplainable occurrences?*

A: I keep a journal of all kinds of writing ideas — like a sewing basket, it has buttons and threads of thought that I might find useful one day in my writing. Unexplainable occurrences are certainly a part of my journal.

Q: *Is it true you write in your laundry room?*

A: I write in my laundry room because it has no phone, and nobody else in the family wants to be in there. When my kids were growing up and the house was very noisy, sometimes I put on the washing machine or dryer when I was working. I found the sloshing and humming sounds were good for thinking.

Q: *Are you skilled at working with pentominoes? Have you gotten a twelve-piecer?*

A: I'm not nearly as skillful at making large rectangles with a set of pentominoes as many third-graders I've known. Yes, I've gotten a twelve-piecer — after an embarrassing amount of time!

Q: *When did you realize you wanted to be a writer?*

A: I knew I wanted to be a writer by the time I was eight or nine. I wrote poetry when I was in college, then two books of oral history, which is nonfiction. I wasn't brave enough to write fiction until I was in my forties, but it's so much fun that I can't imagine doing anything else now.

Q: *What advice do you have for young writers?*

A: To be patient, listen to your own ideas, and expect writing to be messy. Figuring out exactly what you want to say and how you want to say it is sometimes a slow process, with lots of rethinking and rewriting. But I also believe that being a writer is one of the most satisfying things a person can do. What a thrill when the words come out on the page and you know they're just right!

Q: *What do you do when you're not writing?*

A: When I'm not writing, I like to be with my family (we laugh a lot), take walks in the neighborhood, visit all the bookstores, curl up and read, travel, wander around in museums, and sometimes cook. I've found that ideas for writing come from all kinds of unpredictable places.

Q: *So, Blue, will there be another book about Calder and Petra?*

A: Calder and Petra weren't quite finished with me yet, so I'm working on another book set in Hyde Park, during the spring and summer of Calder and Petra's sixth-grade year. A Frank Lloyd Wright building, the Robie House, is a part of the plot, as well as a Hitchcock movie, an H.G.Wells novel, ghosts, and Fibonacci numbers . . . and Hyde Park is hot, often steamy, deserted. . . . The ingredients in this second mystery are quite different.

Q&A with Brett Helquist

Q: *What was the most challenging part of creating the art for* Chasing Vermeer?
A: The hardest part was finding a way to hide the pentomino code into the pictures. I didn't want to make the code too difficult or too easy to figure out.

Q: *What kind of research did you do for the project?*
A: I spent a few days in Chicago with Blue Balliett exploring the neighborhood described in the book. The architecture is very important to the story, so I thought it was necessary to see it for myself. I also looked at some books about Vermeer, and just for fun I played with some pentominoes.

Q: *Who's your favorite painter? Why?*
A: My favorite painter is N.C. Wyeth. His pictures are full of pirates, cowboys, and knights, all the things I love. His paintings tell great stories, they are full of adventure.

Q: *You read a lot of comic books as a kid. Do you still?*
A: I read them sometimes. I like *Hellboy* and *Bone*.

Q: *Any advice for aspiring young artists?*
A: Learn how to draw very well. I know this sounds obvious but it really is the most important thing. Drawing is a skill that should be studied and practiced just like learning to play a musical instrument. I keep a sketchbook and try to draw every day. I also recommend reading and learning how to tell stories. Illustration, after all, is just telling stories with pictures.

Create — Your — Own —
U:2 P:1 L:1 T:2 P:1 V:2 — L:1 L:2 N:1 P:1

Do you like sharing secrets with a friend? Well, then maybe you and your friend need a secret code. Calder and Tommy used pentominoes and the numbers one, two, and three to create their secret code. How will you make yours? Here are a few ideas to get you thinking.

Try substituting the twenty-six letters of the alphabet with the numbers one through twenty-six. Just to throw any snoopers off the trail, count *backwards*: A=26, B=25, C=24, and so on. Can you decipher this? 4-19-26-7 26-9-22 8-12-14-22 12-7-19-22-9 18-23-22-26-8?

Try making a code using a combination of shapes and numbers. One way to do this is to create a grid similar to Calder and Tommy's. Run the shapes (as many or as few as you'd like) down the side and the numbers along the top. Then fill in the alphabet either up and down or across the rows. In this code, A=1□, B=2□, K=4 △, and Z=5○.

	1	2	3	4	5	6	7
□	A	B	C	D	E	F	G
△	H	I	J	K	L	M	N
☆	O	P	Q	R	S	T	U
○	V	W	X	Y	Z		

Once you and your friend have your own secret code, grab a postcard or some notepaper to write a message that only the two of you can read!

Make Your Own Pentominoes

Do you like puzzles? Do you like making stuff? Try making your own pentominoes! Here's how:

You'll need a pencil, a ruler, a highlighter or crayon, a 6" × 10" piece of thin cardboard (perhaps the cover of an old spiral notebook), and a pair of scissors.

1. Each of the twelve pentominoes in a set is made from 5 equal size squares. To make your set, begin by making a grid. Starting at a corner of your 6" × 10" piece of cardboard, make a tic-mark every inch along each edge of your rectangle.
2. Use your ruler and pencil to draw straight dark lines connecting the tic-marks top to bottom, then side to side, to create your grid.
3. Following the diagram below, outline each five-square pentomino with your highlighter or crayon.

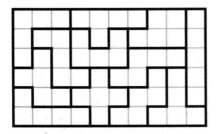

4. Now you're ready to cut out your pentominoes. Cut straight along the highlighted lines.

Voilà! You now have twelve pentominoes and you're ready to play.

How I Draw, with Brett Helquist

When Brett Helquist began the illustrations for *Chasing Vermeer*, he didn't just sit down and draw the cover, the map, and the twenty-four pictures inside the book. First he had to decide what the characters looked like. Blue Balliett describes Calder and Petra in the text (she writes, for example, "he always looked like he'd just woken up," and she "had a fierce triangle of hair"), but Brett still had a lot of work to do. Think about how many people you know with brown curly hair or sleepy eyes. Even with these features in common, they are each unique. Through trial and error and many, many sketches, Brett arrived at the characters in this book. Here are a few of those sketches.

Every piece of art has a skeleton that starts with a few lines.

One way to determine if a person's head is drawn too big or
too small for their body is through proportions: For young
people, the body is usually five heads high; adults' bodies are
generally seven heads high.

Illustrators often have to draw the same character over and over again with different expressions.

Sometimes it's helpful to make notes in the margin, like "too much forehead" or "6 heads tall." With each small adjustment, the character begins to come to life.

What Is It?

Its strength comes from being whole, but its parts are fragile. Its outside is mostly the color of autumn leaves — umber, gold, red, yellow — while its insides have no colors at all. It is smaller than a pizza box but holds thousands of letters. It can be used once or over and over. It weighs about as much as three peanut butter and jelly sandwiches. It holds a mystery, four codes, many pictures, and a secret message.

Can you guess what it is? Guess a few times . . .

Answer (see p. 57 for Calder and Tommy's code):
W:1 V:2 — W:1 U:2 — V:2 V:1 P:1 — I:1 L:2 L:2 Y:1 — W:1 I:2 — F:3 L:2 W:2 T:2 — V:1 F:1 I:2 N:1!

Your turn! Choose an item — maybe something at home — that feels like a work of art to you. Describe this object without saying what it is. Then see if your friends and family can guess what it is you've described. Did you stump them?

Ways of Seeing

Have you ever been to a museum or art gallery and felt bored? Not really sure what it is you're supposed to be "looking at"? Well, breaking down a piece of art to its core elements — sort of like breaking down a recipe by ingredients — is a great place to start. You can focus on the artist's technique: How is the medium (paint, pencil, pastel, ink, etc.) applied? Check out the composition — that's the placement of the picture's elements. Look at the colors used. How do the artist's color choices affect the mood or emotions of the artwork? Focus on the subject matter — what is being depicted? (Sometimes the choice is abstract.) Each element can be seen individually or as part of a whole. You may like one aspect of a painting or sculpture but not another. However you choose to look at art, just keep looking; there are many ways of seeing.

A trip to a museum can be a treasure hunt or a game. When you look at Vermeer's paintings — or any other artist's work — you might want to look for patterns or recurring ideas. Does the artist paint one item over and over? What is it? Are his or her color choices always the same? Calder, Petra, and the rest of Ms. Hussey's class searched for letters in paintings (even though they didn't have much luck). Choose a different item (for example, apples, teacups, or tulips) and see if you can find it in various artists' work. How do different artists treat the same object? Do any patterns emerge? Keep track.

Chase Down a Vermeer

Vermeer is thought to have painted thirty-five paintings, but he didn't sign them all. To this day, there is debate as to the authenticity of some of the paintings attributed to him. The original paintings can be found in museums around the world, so depending on where you live, perhaps you can see one for yourself. If not, there are many great books where you can examine the reproductions. Whether you're admiring one of Vermeer's paintings on a wall or a reproduction of one in a book or on a Web site, be sure to look at his technique, composition, color, and subject matter.

For a complete list of the locations of each of Vermeer's paintings and links to view the paintings, go to (www.scholastic.com/afterwords). You also might want to explore *Vermeer: The Complete Works* by Arthur K. Wheelock (published by Harry N. Abrams, Inc., 1997).

Special Sneak Preview of

THE WRIGHT 3

BLUE BALLIETT'S

exciting sequel to

CHASING VERMEER

CHAPTER ONE INVISIBLE

⊞ ⊞ ⊞ On the morning of June 3, the mason climbed carefully to the highest level of the roof. He was alone, and looked around happily: spring in Chicago, a day with no wind, and a world that was all new leaves. Smells of black earth and lilac mingled with children's voices from the school down the street, and he felt suddenly lucky.

I'm young and alive and almost invisible up here in the trees, he found himself thinking, and then shook his head at such a strange idea. Turning his attention back to the famous terra-cotta roof, he ran his hand along the chimney. A chunk of brick broke loose, rattling downward, and landed with a distant *ping* on the terrace below.

At that moment he lost his footing. Startled, he flung his arms out for balance. Had he been standing on a loose tile? Was this an earthquake? He listened for car alarms, but the street below him was quiet. There was a second, longer shudder, and he thought he saw the roof itself rippling toward him in quick, irregular lines. The building seemed to have come alive, twitching in the irritable way an animal does when it wants to get rid of a fly. The mason staggered to the left. Muttering "What the —" he stumbled back to the right and sank to his knees.

His fall was sudden, a whirl of blue and branches and panic. He knew he would hit concrete. Copper gutters flashed by, and he landed heavily on the balcony outside the dining room. From where he lay, triangles in the stained glass panels above his head flashed like sharp teeth. He struggled to breathe, but felt as if a huge weight had landed on his chest; he was suffocating.

Invisible, his frightened mind whispered, you're invisible *now*. The house was empty and he knew he was hidden from the street, and he wondered if he would die before he was found. In the seconds before his vision melted into blackness, he thought he heard a high voice, the shrill command of a child, but he couldn't quite make out the words. Was it "Stay away!" or "Stay and play"?

CHAPTER TWO   MURDER
IN THE CLASSROOM

⊞ ⊞ ⊞ Tommy Segovia looked out the window of his classroom and chewed on a thumbnail that was already raw. He had been away for a year, and everything had changed—his home, his best friend, his teacher. Coming back to Chicago that June, he felt oddly like a ghost.

His old house on Harper Avenue, in the south side community known as Hyde Park, had been painted a green that reminded him of unripe tomatoes. The bushes in front where he and his friend Calder Pillay had buried treasures—a rusty switchblade found by the train tracks, a dead balloon filled with bottle caps, a Cracker Jack box of cicada shells—had vanished. White flowers now puffed outward in a stiff circle around the foundation. Tommy felt sorry for his house: It reminded him of a birthday cupcake that had fallen upside down.

Even Calder seemed different. Tommy always pictured him with his hair squashed in a straight-up position, fresh from sleep and no brushing, and at least one patch of dried food on his face. Calder's sneakers were tied most mornings now, and he'd brushed his teeth. He still carried a set of pentominoes in his pocket, but they weren't the flat, plastic ones that Tommy remembered. These were three-dimensional and made from small orange cubes. The pieces felt slippery and looked shiny, and you could almost see your reflection in the P. They made a different sound when Calder stirred them around in his pocket, more of a soft clatter than a sharp clack. Tommy liked the old sound better.

Calder lived across the street from Tommy's old house, and had made a new friend on Harper Avenue while Tommy was gone. Her name was Petra Andalee. She had curly hair, thick glasses, and small, quick hands. Her eyes made him think of an exotic monkey he had always admired at the Lincoln Park Zoo. He didn't think she'd like that idea, and he didn't know if he did, either. They had accidentally collided yesterday on the stairs at school, and he noticed that she wasn't as bony as Calder, and she smelled like lemons.

They were all sixth graders now at the University School, and all twelve years old. Their teacher was new and young, and her name was Ms. Isabel Hussey. She had long hair and lots of earrings, and yesterday she had worn pajamas. Tommy didn't think she looked like a teacher at all, but to his amazement, the class paid close attention to her. He tried, but there was so much to stare at and think about that it was hard to do anything else.

The classroom walls were covered with newspaper articles and odd quotes and paper footprints of all sizes. Appearing in every color of the rainbow, the feet marched clockwise around the room, just under the ceiling, as if a kid were walking parallel to the floor. Calder explained to Tommy that each time you read a book, you wrote the title and author inside a tracing of your own foot and cut it out of construction paper.

Books were not Tommy's thing, but looking at all those feet made him want to see his own up there, too. He began wondering what he'd read during his year away that he could write down, but he couldn't remember even one title. How had Ms. Hussey gotten the feet up there? He pictured her balancing on top of bookshelves and on the tray under the blackboard. No wonder she didn't wear skirts much.

One of the quotes Tommy first noticed was on the wall at the front of the room. It said, in black capitals on red paper:

"ART IS THE MOST EFFECTIVE MODE OF
COMMUNICATION THAT EXISTS."
— John Dewey, *Art as Experience*

Tommy knew John Dewey had started the University School at least a hundred years ago. He knew he was a smart guy, but he'd never heard Dewey was big on art. This quote seemed kind of silly. After all, art didn't actually *say* anything.

Another quote said:

"ALL THERE IS TO THINKING . . .
IS SEEING SOMETHING NOTICEABLE
WHICH MAKES YOU SEE SOMETHING
YOU WEREN'T NOTICING,
WHICH MAKES YOU SEE SOMETHING
THAT ISN'T EVEN VISIBLE."
— Norman Maclean, *A River Runs Through It*

This was hard to puzzle out but cool anyway, kind of like an optical illusion tucked into an illustration. Tommy loved looking at one particular page in every issue of the kids' magazines at his dentist's office: the trick page that had teapots or lizards or fish hidden in a line drawing.

He liked the idea of seeing things you can't really see.

Tommy knew from Calder that Ms. Hussey and her class had spent most of last fall investigating art. He was secretly glad he'd missed it, until something happened in December: Calder and this girl Petra stumbled on a big discovery. They found a stolen painting, a famous one by a guy named Vermeer. Newspapers wrote articles that praised Calder and Petra for being extraordinary detectives. This hurt for a couple of reasons: one, Tommy was a far better finder than his friend Calder, and two, before this, they had done everything important together. If he hadn't been away, Tommy was sure it would have been Calder and him who recovered the painting, and recovered it in even less time. There was no doubt about it— he'd missed some major glory.

And then there was a horrible twist to the whole painting adventure: Just over a year ago, Tommy's mom had met and married a man who had been the reason the three of them moved to New York last summer. He had seemed like a decent guy at first. That man, Tommy's stepfather, had played a part in the theft and then died of a heart attack before he could be arrested. Although Tommy had been told that no one blamed him or his mom for the crime, it was embarrassing that everyone in Hyde Park knew, and Tommy hated the idea that people might feel sorry for them.

They had planned to move back to Hyde Park during summer vacation, but Tommy's mom had been offered her old job at the University Library, plus a small raise, if they moved in June. Because she was back at work, he was back in the classroom. So here he was with ten days left to the school year, and not a lot of time for making things better. He frowned and tried again to pay attention.

The class was now looking at buildings. The week before Tommy returned, they'd visited the Sears Tower and Frank Gehry's new pavilion in Millennium Park. The class hadn't agreed yet on whether either structure was a piece of art. Ms. Hussey asked lots of questions, like, Is a building a piece of art when you can't see all of it at the same time? Can a building be a piece of art on the outside, but not on the inside and vice versa? She was usually calm and curious, but on this particular morning, Tommy thought she'd gone a little crazy.

She was holding a newspaper article in her hand, and hardly seemed to notice that the class was in front of her. Shaking her head slowly, as if whatever she was thinking about was impossible to believe, she said softly, "Plunder in the name of salvation." Then she repeated it, spitting out the syllables as if they were something disgusting that had gotten into her mouth. All rustling and chair-squeaking stopped.

She waved the article at arm's length. Her voice now dangerously cheerful, she added, "Or perhaps a better term is murder."

The class was silent.

Murder?

Unleash the secrets within.

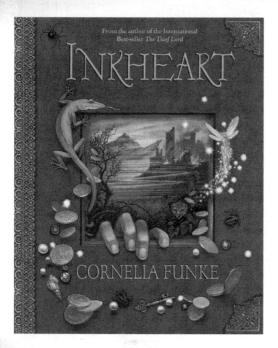

Meggie and her father Mo share a peaceful life together. But one evening a mysterious stranger forces Mo to reveal his extraordinary gift—a gift Meggie may also possess. Discover their remarkable secret—and how changes their lives forever—in this thrilling adventure.

ON THE RUN

TWO FUGITIVE KIDS.
ONE BIG MISSION. THE CHASE IS ON!

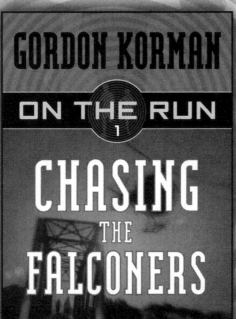

GORDON KORMAN

ON THE RUN
1

CHASING
THE
FALCONERS

■ SCHOLASTIC

The Falconers are facing life in prison—unless their children, Aiden and Meg, can follow a trail of clues to prove their parents' innocence. Aiden and Meg are on the run, and they must use their wits to make it across the country, facing plenty of risks along the way!

■ SCHOLASTIC